GW01090800

# Stacey Farr

## and the

# Healing Leaves

by

## Penny Ibbott

For Florence – a truly great reader
of poetry! On Mum & Dad's wedding
Day 13th Sept 2014.
from Penny X.

Pen Press Publishers Ltd

© Penny Ibbott 2006

All rights reserved

No part of this publication may be reproduced,
stored in a retrieval system, or transmitted
in any form or by any means, without
the prior permission in writing of the publisher,
nor be otherwise circulated in any form of binding or
cover other than that in which it is published and without a
similar condition including this condition being imposed
on the subsequent purchaser.

First published in Great Britain by
Pen Press Publishers Ltd
The Old School Road
39 Chesham Road
Brighton BN2 1NB

ISBN 1-905203-94-2
ISBN13: 978-1-905203-94-9

Printed and bound in the UK

A catalogue record of this book is available from
the British Library

Cover design by Jacqueline Abromeit

# Rosie,
## a fade-resistant memory

# Contents

# Chapter One

## THE SOUTHERN BUBBLE

The hotel hung motionless in an almost cloudless sky.

A series of glassy globes, it had been built of materials so fragile in appearance, that it was as if bubbles in a giant cluster were floating through the air for a final few seconds before bursting.

But The Grand World Conference Centre of the Southern Hemisphere was not a flimsy structure, as anyone could see who watched the seemingly endless stream of flying cars – flars, for short – line up before they entered the ornate portals of the hotel's flar-park.

Nobody called it 'The Grand World Conference Centre of the Southern Hemisphere'. It was simply dubbed 'The Bubble' or, because of the identical conference centre in the Northern Hemisphere, 'The Southern Bubble'.

Although it was designed specifically to host prestigious inter-world conferences, The Bubble catered for thousands of ordinary visitors and holiday makers throughout the year. Today though, there was something big going on, (no-one knew quite what – it was all rather hush-hush) and its opulent chambers were occupied by a number of special guests.

In its main hall delegates sat round a long oval table as vast as an ice-rink. Their eyes were respectfully riveted on the chairman, who addressed them in tones that somehow did not match the way he looked. An elderly man of imposing stature, he had a shiny bald head and a huge moustache, to which was fixed a tiny microphone.

In quietly spoken flowery phrases, he welcomed his guests – many of them individually. He hoped they were all in good health, and told them that he and his family were well and sent their greetings to all present. He praised the beauty of such a lovely autumn day, and finally he referred to the circumstances which had brought them together.

"This is a historic occasion," he murmured into his microphone.

"Have you noticed?" whispered one delegate to another, "it's always *historic*...it was historic last time..."

"If you have anything to say, delegate Cheng, would you kindly say it to me?" demanded the chairman, whose ears were very sharp.

Cheng, looking slightly embarrassed, said, "Pardon me, Home-father. I was saying that the last occasion we met was also historic."

"Indeed it was," replied the chairman. "But this time it is even *more* historic! In fact, this occasion is *most* historic!"

"Quite so, Home-father… most historic…" muttered Cheng, who wished that he'd never opened his mouth.

"I will continue." announced the chairman, his gaze sweeping round the table, ensuring that all were paying close attention. "Please tilt your seats back for ceiling visuals." Seats were accordingly adjusted and as images began to flicker across the ceiling, the chairman cleared his throat: "You will see from these latest scenes that our sister planet is ever more in need of help."

Privately, a handful of delegates wondered if the inhabitants of this so-called 'sister planet' wouldn't rather be left to sort out their own mess but none of them dared say so.

As the chairman spoke, a series of what had become known as 'plundered planet' pictures passed across the ceiling. A densely populated city – smog like a shroud lying over its towers and tenements. A sprawling industrial complex with smoke stacks belching noxious clouds. An extensive oil slick, staining sea and shoreline, decimating wildlife. Scarred landscape – a road slashed through a wounded forest.

"And just in case any of you wonder if this so called sister planet's inhabitants wouldn't rather be left to sort out their own mess ..." The words dropped into an embarrassed silence, "... these people really *are* our kin."

And as they looked, there were scenes featuring the planet's people. A child hugging its parents, lovers embracing, two old men laughing, women dancing, a school room full of students, a ball game in a field ... a baby being born.

Then the visuals faded. Seats were tilted forward again. Someone said softly, remembering to address the chairman, "Home-father, perhaps these people could use our healing leaves."

The chairman peered at the delegate beneath brows which were not much smaller than his moustache. "Delegate Nyra – and I say this not just to *you,* Home-daughter, but to every Home-son and daughter in this room – we are not sending the *folia* to Planet Earth at this time. We have sent no plants, no leaves – no seeds." The chairman sat down and continued gently. "And because we have already discussed this at length, every one of you knows why. We mustn't let our sentiments run away with us. We agreed on a plan – every single one of us. And the plan is in action as I speak. First we educate them. Then we send the *folia*."

There was an exchange of glances. Another delegate suddenly asked, "The plan is in action, you said, Home-father. Can we take it that our young scientists have departed?"

"They have indeed. The far-reacher *Star Drifter* left central outport this morning, with eighty children and twenty group leaders on board. They are taking our small-est, most adaptable vehicles – twenty globeringer shoes – four children and one group leader to each shoe. So although they are young and vulnerable, they will be supervised. This is our second attempt to be of assist-ance to Planet Earth. Our positive thoughts and good wishes go with Project EarthAid 2."

"Can I say something Home-father?"

"Delegate Tek," acknowledged the chairman, his ex-pression softening very slightly, as a young man with unruly, sandy coloured hair and a gleam in his pale eyes leapt to his feet.

"I think it's a great idea, all these young ones going to Earth. Ordinary, innocent looking kids! No-one will guess who they *really* are! They'll be able to carry out their assignments and leave – and no-one on earth will know they've been touched."

An elderly woman delegate spoke in censorious tones:

4

"I wonder, delegate Tek, if you would be so enthusiastic about these youngsters risking their lives on an alien – and dangerous – planet, if one of them was your own child?"

"Can't answer that exactly delegate Lana, not having any children of my own. But I should tell you that *one* of those 'youngsters risking their lives' – is my little sister."

## Chapter Two

Tek's twelve-year-old little sister was at that moment juggling with three pieces of fruit. She was being timed by a friend, who was seeing just how long she could keep it up without dropping a piece. She blew a twist of sandy-coloured hair from her eyes and bit her lower lip in concentration.

A cheerful voice came over the public address system. "Okay kids, you have enough time to clean up and get dressed for bed, then it's lights down for the night."

Treo dropped an orange and her friend Mab swooped to pick it up. She showed Treo the timepiece, saying with a smirk, "You still can't keep it going as long as I can!"

"All right. But I can still stand on my head for longer than you, so… *ner!*"

"True!" said Mab. "Now, what other trivial stuff can we get up to, to pass the time?"

"Nothing right now," replied Treo. "Didn't you hear the lady? It's bedtime."

"Yeah, it's just that I'm not tired, that's all."

"Well let's get ready for bed anyway, we can always play Fossfingers in the dark."

"You've got Fossfingers? You never told me!"

"It was a leaving present from Tek."

Mab sighed. "I wish *I* had a generous big brother. I've only got a little one. Mind you, he's very cute – and I think I'm going to miss him more than anyone else in my family." She began to brush her straight, dark hair in front of a mirror. Treo had disappeared into the bathroom. A little later, dressed in their sleep suits, and with the lights in the cabin gradually fading, they sat over a game of Fossfingers. This was a hologram which glowed pleasingly in the dark. A miniature ball game in which players set up as many obstacles as they could to prevent their opponents from scoring a point. Both Treo and Mab were good at the game so neither of them scored for a while. Mab sighed again and looked up. "Treo?"

"Yep?"

"What d'you think of Jay and Brod?"

Treo looked blank.

"*You* know, the two guys assigned to our globeringer team!"

"Oh of course," replied Treo, whose mind was still partly on the game. "Let's see, Jay's the tall, black guy with the crazy sense of humour – I'm glad he's on our team, he'll be fun. But the other one Brod, hmmm... he's cute – I like those big grey eyes – but he's a bit on the quiet side for me."

"Are they older or younger than us?"

"I don't think there's much in it. You're thirteen, so you'll probably be the oldest."

"Hmm."

Both girls stared at the hologram in front of them, their faces reflecting its colours. "Mab?"

"Yep?"

"Are you scared?"

"Nope," Mab frowned. "At least I don't *think* I am! Are you?"

Treo looked up at Mab, her pale eyes wide. Slowly she nodded. "Terrified."

"Just don't be, that's all. We have Ean as our group leader and I would rather have her than anyone else, because she's a well-known specialist in Earth studies. She'll keep us safe."

"She's been to Earth before, hasn't she?"

"Yes, she went with the first EarthAid project. In fact, most of the group leaders who are going with us were on the first EarthAid project. We have all the experts with us. We really will be fine Treo."

Mab almost glared at Treo, as if by doing so she would force her to submerge her fears.

Treo's answer was to yawn. "I guess I must be tired," she murmured. "It's been a long day."

"Yeah. We ought to go to bed. It's going to be another long day tomorrow!"

Treo turned off the game and put it away. Both girls climbed into bed.

"Sleep tight Treo. Sweet dreams eh?"

"You too Mab."

But Mab didn't fall asleep. Her mind was still full of the day's images.

Saying goodbye to mum and dad had been difficult. They'd kept telling her they loved her – as if she didn't know. They kept giving her special fond smiles, and squeezing her arm or her hand until she couldn't wait to get away – to escape from the heavy atmosphere of an imminent farewell. Of course, she would miss them. But there was this special assignment waiting for her – inviting her almost – and she just wanted to go.

*

It had been different with her little brother, Bo. He was only three, and hadn't a clue what she'd be doing. Before he'd settled down to sleep last night, she had spent a last few minutes with him. She had shown him the outfit she would be wearing for the trip. Putting it on, posing in front of him, making funny faces. His fat cheeks had dimpled, then he'd fallen back on his pillow laughing – an infectious, baby laugh that had set Mab giggling.

Her mum was fond of saying that Bo was "the *image* of Mab when *she* was three!" – and had the pictures to prove it. But although the dimples remained, Mab no longer had fat cheeks. The older Mab had a thinner, almost tri-angular face, and that – along with her straight black hair and heavy fringe – made her dark eyes look enormous.

"Play a game! Play a game!" Bo had begged, as she was about to tuck him up for the night. So she'd sat for a while and played a counting game with him. Taking a handful of seeds from a little pot on his windowsill, she'd laid them on the bedcover and begun doing simple sums with them, taking a few away then putting some back.

"Mab! Are you in bed?" her father's voice had called from just outside in the garden.

"Oops!" Mab had scooped the seeds up, and stuffed them in the pocket of her new suit. She'd bent over to kiss Bo goodnight, but he shrank under the cover, and her kiss had landed on the quilt.

*

The *Star Drifter* anchored above Earth just two days later. Early in the morning the girls heard the shields going up. No-one on earth would know they were there. The shield made them impossible to detect.

At breakfast, the children were given their final briefing. They all knew the rules by heart, and one or two of them made bored faces, as their chief instructor, Genno, spoke to them in solemn tones. "Never lose contact with your group leader. Never behave in a way that will draw attention to you. *Never* take anything with you to Earth's surface, and *never* bring anything back!" He paused and looked at each serious face." You are special. We trust you."

A pupil raised his hand. "Please Genno, is it true that the whole expedition would have to be called off if only one little rule was broken?"

Genno gazed over the heads of the children for a moment. "There is no such thing as *only one little rule!* Every single instruction you have been given hinges on the need for us to remain untraced! Remember what you have learnt about INTERCEPT – you know what those letters stand for: **INTER**national **C**ontrol of **E**xtraterrestrial **P**henomena **T**hreat. It is their business to be aware of every little phenomenon that occurs on their planet."

A girl called Sibia asked, "What if things got very difficult and we had to defend ourselves – or re-mask in broad daylight where we might be seen?"

"We understand that events beyond our control can sometimes threaten," Genno replied. Then with a trace of impatience he added, "We have actually been through all this, Sibia." To the company in general, he posed the question: "With whom must we always stay in contact?"

Several voices came back with the answer, "Group leader!"

"And of course, he or she in turn will keep in touch with watch captain. The far-reacher will have a lock on every group – wherever it is on Earth. If a situation arises that you can't deal with, then contact us and we will help." He smiled and walked toward the exit. Then he paused, and turning back to the children once more said, "In the unlikely event that things get out of control... somehow... somewhere... then the mission *would* have to be aborted. It would be a devastating blow, after so much hard work, but it may be the only course for us to take. All I am saying is, YOU CHILDREN ARE SPECIAL – WE TRUST YOU – BE CAREFUL!"

\*

After breakfast the pupils descended in lifts to the launch deck, where they found twenty globeringer shoes lined up in their individual bays, doors open, waiting for their passengers to board. Globeringer shoes – so called because each one resembled a large, white running shoe – were an essential part of Home Planet space travel technology.

At the time a shoe touched down on an alien planet, it was invisible. Once on the planet's surface though, it would require shape and form. This is where 'masking' came in. Built into the shoe's array of defence equipment was a device affectionately known as MAD, which stood for Mask And Defend. Highly sensitive and intelligent, this robot/computer could blend the vehicle into any location where it touched down.

In the case of planet Earth, if it arrived at a roadside, it would change into some kind of road transport – whilst inside everything remained the same. Taking on the form of anything that would make them appear unremarkable in their surroundings, shoes had been known to mask as trains, buses, aircraft, even garden sheds!

However, there was one serious problem that accompanied the arrival of a globeringer shoe on a planet's surface. At the moment of its touchdown and masking, it gave off a massive surge of energy. Energy, discernable as a shower of light, which shimmered like a rainbow before dying down as the shoe cooled. Every time the shoe re-masked, it would produce what its designers called the 'rainbow effect'. Since it was necessary to arrive and depart from Earth without being traced, it was vital that they found a way to conceal the rainbow effect – at least on touchdown.

As the Home Planet technologists experimented, they found that the energy surge didn't show up nearly as much when a shoe touched down in a place where there was an abundance of spraying water. Somehow, the shower of water seemed to mask the shower of light. Then, one day scientists came up with the answer. They discovered the ideal spot where a shoe could land and mask – as a family car perhaps – but the shower of light it released on touchdown would be made almost invisible by masses of water spraying over it.

From then on, it was decided that when globeringer shoes visited Earth, they would only touchdown and mask in selected carwashes.

# Chapter Three

## TOUCHDOWN

It was a Thursday morning in July.

In a service station on the southbound carriageway of the A3 in Hampshire, the carwash had been activated from an outside source. But while the whirling brushes, foam and spray effectively disguised the shoe's touch-down and masking, a drama was taking place on the forecourt.

Two young men had filled up with petrol, then on entering the garage shop apparently to pay for it, had produced guns and ordered the two staff members to hand over whatever money was in the till. There were no other customers in the shop.

One of the staff members had tried resisting and had been knocked unconscious. The other staff member, a young woman, had been easy to overpower and had been dragged into a storeroom at the back and locked in. The criminals had made their getaway, screeching up the highway on smoking tyres. Someone who had merely driven in for petrol, quickly sized up the situation and had called the police, who had arrived in a flurry of blue flashing lights and sirens.

They cordoned the entire service station off and called

an ambulance. Much further up the road a police chase was in progress. But here, an investigation was set in motion. The gentleman who had called the police was politely asked to remain. "I'm sorry, sir, but would you mind answering a few questions?"

"NOT AT ALL!" shouted the motorist, who eased himself out of his van, mopped his brow – it was a sweltering day – and followed the police officer into the cool interior of the shop. He was an elderly shopkeeper named Bascombe, and was returning from a trip to buy supplies for his village hardware store. He'd left his van – the driver's door wide open – parked by one of the pumps.

Mr Bascombe had not experienced so much excitement since the war, and as he began his account, the policeman found himself being bombarded at intervals with little globules of spit. He moved further away, but Mr Bascombe followed him, eagerly leaning towards him and speaking in a super-loud voice, "WHAT NEXT EH, OFFICER? WHAT NEXT? THE THINGS THAT HAPPEN THESE DAYS! POSITIVELY SHOCKING!"

The policeman got his handkerchief out. He was relieved when a junior officer entered the shop. "There was a vehicle going through the car wash during the incident, sir. Do you want to talk to the driver, or shall I?"

"I'll talk to them, Jones!"

"Yes, sir – woman driver and four kids."

"I've finished with this gentleman." He nodded politely at Mr Bascombe. "But we need his name and address. Take care of it!" As he made his way to the door he muttered, "Er, you might need an umbrella Jones..."

*

Inside the shoe there was silence. The group leader, Ean, drummed her fingers on the console. There was obviously going to be some interaction with Earth people here. It was rather sooner than she had planned, but they couldn't drive through the police barrier without causing a bit of a stir.

"What's going to happen, Ean?" Brod asked.

"We'll have to get out. We don't want them peering inside, do we? You must leave the talking to me." The children were only too glad to do as Ean said. They spoke fluent English but felt unanimously that this sudden emergency was best left to the expert.

*

Detective Inspector Baker had got very little from the woman who had come through the car wash. She had been so preoccupied with the whole process, that she hadn't noticed anything suspicious. The kids were no help either. One of the boys had been asleep, the other had been listening to his personal stereo and the two girls had been playing a game. They hadn't seen anything either.

"Well now, just in case you remember something, here is a number on which you can reach me. And of course, I would like a contact name, address and telephone number from you." He stood with his pen poised above a small notebook. He didn't see Ean's sudden look of panic.

"I'm always careful about giving my address away," she said, stalling for time and gazing around as if help might come out of the air. Then, as a high-sided vehicle thundered past, she said, "Stobart."

"Is that with one 'B'?"

Ean told him that it was, and went on to give him an address that was fictitious but not, she hoped, suspect. "And these are my children," she added brightly.

As DI Baker looked surprised, she waded in deeper. "Er, not *my* children exactly. I'm their school teacher. We're on a field trip... learning about different types of... petrol... and which type gives off the most er... pollution." She raised her eyebrows slightly at the children, and they obligingly went over to examine the petrol pumps.

"If this is Earth experience, it sucks. I wish I'd never come!" Treo whispered to Mab, whilst the boys made realistic notes in front of an unleaded petrol pump.

"Me too," answered Mab. "I wish more than anything that I was at home right now." Mab's hand was in the pocket of her outfit. Her hand was clenched into a fist. Inside the fist were eight seeds. Eight seeds of the *Folia Prophylaxis Beautifica* – or healing leaves. The ones she had stuffed into her pocket the night she had kissed her little brother goodbye.

\*

They had been descending in the globeringer shoe, the most dangerous part of their journey. They had all been nervous. Brod had his eyes shut, Jay was clenching his teeth and had *his* eyes shut. Treo had been biting her nails – and Mab had stuffed her hands deep into her jacket pockets. It was at that point that she made the terrible discovery.

She had never removed the seeds from her pocket. She had brought seeds with her to the Earth's surface... *she had broken the rules.*

From then on, Mab was gloomy and preoccupied.. She felt she ought to tell Ean straight away, but was terrified of doing so. The whole mission may have to be aborted! All twenty shoes recalled – because of her! How could she let that happen?

Scared stiff, Mab began to think of possible ways round her dilemma. What if she didn't own up – and her group leader found out? She would be accused of having broken the trust they had in her – and trying to cover up. *What if she somehow secretly got rid of the seeds?* They might still find out – and that would be worse.

*What if she got rid of the seeds and they didn't find out? Was that possible? If she threw the seeds away, could she possibly get away with it? If they were disposed of – and no-one got to know about it – would EarthAid continue as if nothing had happened?*

Mab didn't think this was possible. But when things did not go quite according to plan after touchdown – and they had started to interact with Earth people sooner than they had expected – Mab decided that this was what she was going to do. Even though she felt sneaky and dishonest.

*Somehow she would get rid of the seeds. No-one would know about it, and the mission would continue as planned.*

She saw a yellow bin across the forecourt and read the word "LITTER" on it. It became the focus of her attention.

Treo was muttering: Why did they choose this particular petrol station? Why couldn't Ean foresee that something was going to go wrong? Earth was well known as the violent planet. Crimes were always being committed. It was obvious that one day, someone visiting from Home Planet was going to get caught up in one. How were they going to get out of this?

Of course Mab wasn't listening. They had got to the spot where Mr Bascombe had parked his van – and the driver's door had been left open. A few feet away was the yellow bin, against the shop wall.

"Come on children, let's go!" Ean called them, a note of urgency in her voice. She would be wanting to drive them away to hide up somewhere. A place where they could re-mask – cover their tracks – just in case the police decided to check them out. Mab stared at the bin briefly, then glanced over to where Ean was beckoning. Ean stamped her foot.

"Mab! Come!"

Mab couldn't cross to the yellow bin without arousing suspicion, so she thrust her fist inside the open door of Mr Bascombe's van and dropped the seeds onto the driver's seat.

# Chapter Four

## NIGHTMARE

Ean had been thinking that she couldn't answer any more questions without giving a highly suspicious answer. But then a newspaper reporter and photographer, having parked on the verge outside the petrol station, had removed a section of the police cordon and strolled onto the forecourt as if they owned the place.

This annoyed DI Baker so much, that he strode across to them shouting, "This area is out of bounds – we'll let you know when you can come in."

"Sorry mate." The reporter showed his press card. "We're press – and we've got a job to do!"

There followed a loud argument which brought another couple of policemen running from whatever they had been doing. It was at this point that Ean had called the children. There was now a nice gap in the police tape – and Ean drove through it.

Well, she hadn't broken any law. She should have the freedom to drive away. She had left an address – of sorts. Unless they were very keen to get in touch with her, they would never find out that it didn't exist. Ean was surprised to feel herself trembling. She breathed deeply. She turned to Mab: "Put some music on Mab!"

Mab selected some good, lively music. The atmosphere in the shoe became much lighter and everyone started talking at once.

"That's better!" smiled Ean. " Let's hope the English police are not interested in catching us!" And putting her foot down, they sped away south.

*

Up a winding country lane, which passed through sleepy farmland, in the corner of a remote field, a haystack shimmered with rainbow colours. No-one saw, only a few cows in the next field, and they didn't even stop chewing. Ean, after making sure that the area was still unoccupied, encouraged the four children out of the shoe, suggesting they get some exercise to give them an appetite.

As she prepared food for them, she thought of all the other shoes touching down all around Earth's globe. In other parts of Europe, in North and South America, Africa, Australia and Asia. She wondered if any of them had encountered problems. They were able to contact each other in cases of emergency, but their main line of communication was to the far-reacher. Which reminded her. She must report back and let watch captain know of their safe arrival.

Even as she turned, she noticed a light flashing on the console. She touched the light and it stopped flashing. She informed watch captain, "Hello Globeringer Five, Ean here. Go ahead."

"G5, we've been waiting for your call. Is all OK with you down there?"

"Everything is fine. Touchdown not entirely without mishap though!" and she explained about the hold-up at the service station, the short police interview and their rather hasty departure.

"I take it you've re-masked, Ean?"

"Yes. I don't think there is any danger of the police finding us – we are actually a haystack! MAD seemed to think it was a most appropriate disguise for this particular location!"

There was a short burst of laughter from the watch captain, then he said, "We have a lock on you, G5. I believe you are heading south for your assignment, aren't you?"

"That's right. Of course, we'll have to re-mask again before we move. A haystack driving along an English highway might cause a few heads to turn!" This time they both laughed.

"All right Ean. If you are in need of any assistance, call us – or route a message through the nearest shoe. As you know, one touched down in France this morning. Take care and have a successful visit. Out."

The meal Ean had prepared was tasty, although she ate hardly anything because she wasn't hungry. Mab and Brod cleared away and they all settled down to write their journals. Homefolk are careful keepers of hand-written records. As soon as they are old enough to grasp a writing stick, they are taught the first simple strokes of hand-writing. All of them are left-handed. (When there is a great volume of writing to be done, they have the muse writer, which projects the writer's thoughts straight to screen or page – the text appearing in a font and colour to suit the mood of the writer.)

As Ean sat thinking about the next day, all she could hear was the soft scratch of writing sticks, as four heads bent to the task of writing down the day's events. And the day had certainly been eventful. They were all – herself included – very tired. Even so, she must set her personal alarm to wake her during the quietest, darkest hour of the night. That would be the safest time to re-mask the shoe – and start out for their final destination.

But later, when the children had lengthened their seats and were fast asleep, Ean – still awake – began to tremble again. It couldn't be because she was afraid – after all, they were masked and it was dark – they were safe for a good few hours yet. She also felt abnormally warm, so she checked the air conditioning. Cool, fresh air was filtering through hidden ducts. So why did she feel hot and shivery? Why was she so thirsty? She got up – unsteady on her feet – and made herself a cool drink.

As with all the other group leaders, Ean had been hand-picked for her qualities. Courageous, enterprising, and with good decision-making skills, she also possessed a natural gift when it came to working with people – especially children. Being a group leader for this trip to Earth was a huge responsibility. Her priority, of course, was the security and well-being of the children. They must work as a team to fulfil their mission, but above all things, they must be returned safe and sound to Home Planet. As she got back into her bed, Ean felt an uncharacteristic surge of panic. She was feeling distinctly unwell. Is this how coming to Earth had affected her? How could she supervise and care for her young team if she felt like this? Before she lay down her eyes rested briefly on each of the sleeping children.

Brod was on his side, his face turned away from her. But she was very familiar with that mop of light brown hair, the serious grey eyes, which seemed to reflect his nature. Thoughtful and sensitive, he had a reserve which sometimes made it hard for others to befriend him. He had a tendency to think out his personal problems and then act on them without consulting any of his friends or teachers. This was a worry to Ean, who had constantly encouraged him to either confide in her, or – if not too personal – discuss his feelings with his immediate group. Ean remembered how his shyness had made it difficult for him when he'd had to give a talk to the class about his specialist subject, which was animal management.

"Just think about your love of animals, Brod," she had encouraged him, "and when you look at your audience don't see it as a crowd, but as a bunch of individuals that you have come to know and like. You'll be fine!" He had struggled at first, blushing and stammering through the material he had prepared. After a while though, he had warmed to his subject, even causing his audience to laugh on a couple of occasions.

Jay was just about as opposite to Brod as a person could get. Ean found herself smiling, in spite of feeling ill, as Jay said something in his sleep and then laughed. The tallest of the group, Jay was ironically the youngest. He was the outgoing one, the extrovert – the group clown. A perceptive boy, he was ever alert to what was going on around him, picking up the changes in mood, either of a group or of an individual. He was also quick to react to such variations in emotional climate. This gave him a sympathetic and caring nature. If Jay couldn't joke you out of an unhappy frame of mind, thought Ean affectionately, he would fling an arm around you and lovingly coax you out of it. His specialist field was healing.

Treo was curled up like a cat – her cover had fallen onto the floor. Ean would normally have picked it up and spread it over her again, but somehow it was too much of an effort. What a mixed up personality Treo was! She came from a family whose genius was well documented. Her brother, Tek, was on the globeringer development team, having contributed significantly to its research. Like her brother, she was extremely bright, had a head for figures, and a light touch when it came to handling complex equipment. But Treo was also of a nervous disposition. Because of this, the selection board had nearly left her off the team, but her test results had been outstanding and it was decided she would be a definite asset. Her specialist field was engineering.

All Ean could see of Mab was the top of her head with its dark hair. She wondered if she was imagining it, but Mab had somehow seemed troubled since the shoe had touched down. That was unusual for Mab. Small for her age, her personality made up for her lack of stature. She was enterprising and smart, but her honesty and sense of humour softened what might otherwise have been a bossy nature. During all their training, it was Mab who always seemed to have an answer to everything. She was the one who had written the most, answered up the most, and given the longest talks. Ean grinned. Mab. A bit of a know-it-all, but with a heart of gold. Her specialist field was mental science.

They were a great bunch of kids. Ean had grown very fond of them over the weeks and months of training, and now their assignment had begun, she felt fiercely protective of them. Would she get them safely back home? Would they, in spite of their rigorous preparation, leave traces? Would they fall into the clutches of Intercept? She must watch them closely. Ean began to shiver again.

Intercept. **INTER**national **C**ontrol of **E**xtraterrestrial **P**henomena **T**hreat was planet Earth's agency for the detection of extraterrestrial life. They had the most advanced equipment for an Earth agency, although primitive by Home Planet standards. Nevertheless, they were ambitious hunters. As their name suggested, they regarded any extraterrestrial life-form as a threat and their attempts to control it would include – if given the chance – capture and experimentation.

As Ean lay back to sleep, her bed suddenly became an operating table. She realised she was in the sterile atmosphere of an experimental lab. Shadowy, masked figures approached her. Their white overalls bore an emblem – a globe with the Intercept flash across it like a No Entry sign. They held gleaming, sharp instruments. A muffled voice spoke: "They look like us – but do they have the same anatomy? Where shall we start cutting?"

Ean, who was now well and truly into her nightmare, opened her mouth to cry out but all she could manage was a feeble croak. She tried bringing her hands up to defend herself but her arms were secured to her sides with metal clamps. She brought all her concentration to bear. Could she control them with her mind? "*No, no, NO!*" she tried to yell. Then she was suddenly awake – and sat up gasping.

"It had been a nightmare! Just a bad dream... thank goodness..." and as she put her hands to her thumping heart, she realised she was damp with sweat.

After that, Ean was too uncomfortable – and too scared – to try to sleep again. She heard it start to rain in the early hours of Friday morning, and listened as the downpour continued into the brightening day.

# Chapter Five

**SEEDS**

As she and her younger brother were about to leave for school on that same Thursday morning in July, Stacey Farr's dad told her, "Pop into Bascombes on your way home from school, Stacey. I need a box of screws."

Stacey was pushing her feet into her trainers. "Can you write it down dad, 'cos last time I forgot the size and how many you wanted!"

"Already done!" he replied, handing her an envelope, which she stuffed down the side of her bag. "The money's in there too, so don't lose it!"

Later that day as they dawdled home from school, Stacey was thinking about the maths exam her class had taken that morning. She normally liked maths, but had found this one difficult and was worried that she wouldn't keep up her record of good marks. She had forgotten all about her errand, but as they were passing the hardware store, Jonathan piped up: "Don't forget dad's box of screws, Stace!"

"I hadn't forgotten Jon. I'm not stupid!" she snapped, turning immediately aside into the shop, where a bell jangled loudly above the door. She fished around in her bag for the envelope dad had given her, while Jon walked around peering at things and picking them up.

Finally Stacey found the rather screwed up envelope in her pocket and handed the note and money over to Mr Bascombe, who had been watching Jonathan like a hawk. He pushed the box of screws across the counter to Stacey and gave her the change from her dad's fiver, putting the coins inside the envelope. As they were leaving the shop, she stopped by the flower pots and garden tools. She wanted a small watering can for her garden. Dad's was too big and heavy. There was a small plastic one, reduced to one ninety-nine, she would ask dad to get it for her.

Then she caught sight of the seeds.

Of course there were the usual packets of seeds and a few trays of seedlings. But there was also a tray with an odd mixture of seeds in it. When she asked him, Mr Bascombe said they were an assortment of leftovers, which he was selling off cheap. Stacey thought they looked more like something he'd swept up off the floor.

But as she examined them, she saw that there were a few which were like no seeds she had ever seen. They were the size of large beans, and the colour of their skins was.... Stacey could only think of it as oil on the surface of a puddle – swirling, rainbow-like. She counted them. There were eight. She picked one up. There was a tiny split down its side. Whatever strange plant they contained, the seeds were ready to sprout. They should be planted as soon as possible.

She didn't like talking to Mr Bascombe any more than she had to. He was rather deaf and spoke very loudly all the time. That wasn't so bad, but he seemed always to have an overload of spit, and as he leant toward the person he was talking to, he would spray them generously. Still, she decided to ask if he knew what the seeds in the tray were.

"BIT OF A SURPRISE PACKAGE REALLY!" he shouted, spit flying everywhere. "PLANT 'EM AND SEE WHAT YOU GET!"

Using the sleeve of her T-shirt to wipe her cheek, Stacey asked how much they were.

"OOH LET'S SEE, GIVE US FIFTY PENCE YOUNG LADY – AND WE'LL CALL IT A DEAL."

She took a fifty pence piece from the change in the envelope and handed it over.

The seeds were shaken gently into a brown paper bag and Mr Bascombe folded it over, securing it with sticky tape."SOME OF THOSE ARE SUNFLOWER SEEDS – YOU'LL NEED TO PLANT 'EM IN POTS!"

Stacey took a step or two backwards as all the 'S' sounds produced a spit explosion.

"THEY'LL NEED WATERING! – MIND YOU WATER 'EM GOOD AND PROPER!" Stacey felt that they'd probably already had a good watering.

Jonathan held the box of screws and Stacey stuffed the bag of seeds into the pocket of her shorts as they crossed the road hand in hand, which Stacey insisted they do. Jonathan thought this was stupid – he was quite old enough at six to cross by himself. But Stacey was very bossy and at nearly eleven, had ways of making him do as she said. As soon as they were on the other side, he wrenched his hand out of Stacey's and ran on home.

She mooched along, making a mental note where to plant her new seeds. Dad would have to give her a bit more space, because she already had lettuces and radishes growing in her vegetable section. The flower section was full of bizzy lizzies and petunias, and she had honeysuckle growing up the fence. All the flowers were of the soft, summery sort, and she didn't want them to be pushed out of the way by something that might grow into a tree!

She gazed after Jonathan's disappearing figure and watched as he sped round the corner into the road where they lived. Nothing got him down. Sandy haired and with a sprinkling of freckles, his sunny nature was reflected in his face – which wore a habitual expression of pleased surprise. Problems puzzled rather than depressed him. Stacey supposed he was too young to have anything trouble him for long. She wished she was like that.

Maybe she was too old – too sensitive – but problems lodged themselves inside her head and tended to stay. The most obvious and difficult one to deal with was her mum's disappearance. Stacey quickly tucked that one away. She didn't want to think about it now. She knew it would re-surface later. Another bugbear was the way she looked. She didn't possess Jonathan's gentle "gingery-ness". With bright red hair, eyes of vivid blue and a face smothered with freckles, she felt she was a loser before she even opened her mouth. And when she did...

Well, the boys in her class called her the Volcano – and not just because of her hair. She was quick to lose her temper. Being teased about her appearance made her flare up. At the same time though, she stuck up fiercely for her friends and was especially protective of Jonathan. With both hands, she flattened the hair which sprang from her scalp like an unruly fountain. It had been left to grow since mum had gone. She sighed, wishing it was a nice, dull brown.

Suddenly she remembered the seeds she had just bought and her mood lifted. She would plant them after tea. Working on her own personal piece of garden was something she loved. She thought of the eight weird, rather beautiful seeds which looked so ready to grow, and felt a tingle of excitement. What, she wondered, would they turn out to be?

*

They had egg and chips for tea – chips were dad's speciality. Stacey admired her dad. He could have said awful things about mum going off and leaving them – but he never did. He just tried to keep things going, being brisk and cheerful – never giving the impression that he was sorry for himself. The problem was, that 'brisk and cheerful' sometimes got on Stacey's nerves.

Dad didn't seem to know what 'sensitive' meant. It showed up in the way he washed their clothes – often coloured things with white ones – on a hot wash. Nearly all her white socks were now pink – and he still made her wear them. It showed up in the way he sometimes cooked their meals. He was very good at chips, but meat – often burnt – would be 'all right with some gravy'. An overcooked fruit pie would be 'fine with some ice-cream or custard'. When she was feeling depressed, her dad would say, "Cheer up girl, for goodness sake. You look like a wet weekend!" – when she would have given anything for a long, cosy chat. Stacey loved her dad, but she badly missed mum.

After tea, they all ended up in the back garden. Dad was on the patio, sanding down an old table, which someone wanted resurfacing. All Stacey could see was the top of his head. He had the same light, sandy hair as Jonathan – the same blue-grey eyes. Stacey stood for a moment, flattening her hair, wondering why she hadn't inherited her dad's colouring!

Jonathan asked if he could help. He was given a piece of sandpaper and told to start rubbing down the table legs. Stacey wandered over to her plot. Dad had given her an extra patch of garden. It was not next to her other patch, but was a long strip running from the fence to the compost heap. It stank, but she knew anything planted near the compost heap would grow well, so she didn't complain.

She picked out the weird seeds. Because no-one could tell her what they were, there was only one way of finding out. She dropped them into holes about five centimetres deep and forty centimetres apart, covering them with earth and then watering them. She used dad's watering can, staggering across the garden, slopping water all over her legs and feet. Feeling pleased with her work, she stood there with muddy hands and knees, watching the water slowly sink into the dark brown earth. She thought of the seeds feeling cosy in their bed – and being glad of something to drink. And she imagined them beginning to sprout.

*

As she was about to go up to bed, her dad put a pile of clean, folded laundry in her arms. "Put this lot away, will you Stacey? And I mean put it away! Don't just dump Jonathan's stuff on his bed like you did last time. It'll end up on the floor. G'night love!" He gave her a peck on the cheek.

The light was off in Jon's room when she went in there but he was awake – shooting aliens out of the sky from underneath his duvet. She tossed his socks and pants into an already open top drawer and told him he should be asleep, before going and putting her dad's things away in his room. Dad's drawer was almost as untidy as Jon's, and it was as she was cramming a pair of socks down the side of it, that she found the letter.

It was addressed to her dad – "My Dearest Peter," in her mum's handwriting. Stacey pulled the page out of the envelope. She knew she shouldn't really read it but she was going to anyway.

> *Darling,*
>
> *I am crying as I write. I never wanted to leave you and the children under such a black cloud. I wanted to be able to depart with dignity and a loving farewell. But the last time I saw your face, it was furious and withdrawn. You were not going to give an inch, were you? And if you don't understand, then the children certainly won't. So before I leave tonight, I shall go in and kiss their sleeping faces...*

That was as far as Stacey got. She heard her dad get up and move around. She didn't wait to see if he was going to come upstairs. Stuffing the letter back in its envelope, she replaced it in the drawer and sneaked back to her room.

She lay awake for ages that night, her thoughts churning round like clothes in a washing machine. All the old questions kept repeating themselves. One day, mum had gone to work early as usual and had just never come home. Why did she go? And where? She had tried to explain to Stacey – and even Jonathan, that there was something special she had to do, something extremely important. She had said that she would be gone for some time – but that she would be back. They thought she meant a weekend, or a week. Jonathan had said, "OK mum, see you when you get back!" – given her an absent-minded kiss and gone to bed. Stacey had hugged her briefly, disturbed at the heavy atmosphere. But it wasn't a weekend. It wasn't a week.

Mum had been gone for a year. Stacey couldn't help but wonder if she had fallen in love with another man – but there was no clue. Anyway, that line of thought was too painful, so Stacey got angry instead. How dare mum leave them like that? And then never get in touch with them? She thought that it must be because her parents had parted in such anger. But what had her *children* done, that she never called them – or wrote them a letter?

Realising she was thirsty, she got up and went down to the kitchen for a drink of blackcurrant juice. As she added water from the tap, she saw through the window that there was something in the middle of the lawn. It looked like a football someone had kicked over the fence. The ball moved, and she grinned. It was a hedgehog. She unlocked the back door and tip-toed out into the garden, watching as the hedgehog snuffled along, finally disappearing under a bush.

The night air was full of perfume – honeysuckle, night

scented stock, sweet peas. An owl called softly. She walked in her bare feet over the cool grass. She could just make out where she had watered her garden. The young lettuces showed up against the dark, damp soil. She liked to imagine they were her children. Every growing thing in her garden had been looked after and carefully watered.

She looked at her new strip by the compost heap. There was no dampness there. Surprised, she crouched down and felt the earth. It was as dry as a bone – even slightly warm. But she had watered it so thoroughly! She got an old saucepan from the shed and scooping water from the water butt, soaked the area again, going back three or four times. She returned the saucepan to the shed and as she walked back into the house, imagined the seeds slurping away happily. She felt content. Creeping back upstairs, she snuggled under her duvet and fell into a deep sleep.

In the very early hours of the morning before it got light, it started to rain. She didn't hear it, but when she got up, she knew it must have been raining for some time as there were puddles everywhere.

Because she had been so long finally getting to sleep during the night, it was difficult to get going that morning. Dad kept nagging her to hurry up, and Jon had lost his sports kit so dad nagged him about that. The car wouldn't start. So although it was raining, they had to walk to school, arriving late – and wet.

## Chapter Six

### WHERE IS MUM?

Friday turned out to be a rotten day for the two Farr children. They made a bad start by arriving late for school. Dad had told Stacey that she would have to explain, as he had to stay at home and find out what was wrong with the car.

"Car wouldn't start eh, Stacey?" her form teacher commented loudly in front of an already seated class. "Couldn't get out of bed more likely!"

Everyone laughed as Stacey walked red-faced to her seat. The fact that it was partly true made her feel even more embarrassed.

Her friend Gemma, feeling sorry for her, passed her a peppermint under the desk. "You look half drowned Stace!" she hissed.

"I *am* half drowned!" Stacey cracked the peppermint between her teeth, watching to make sure that sir hadn't heard. He carried on writing on the blackboard.

Gemma whispered, "You know you always wanted straight dark hair, Stace?"

"Yeah?" Stacey, still chewing, reduced the mint to a crumble and swallowed.

"Well, you're so wet, that your hair *is* straight and dark!"

Stacey pulled a piece of her hair round in front of her eyes and squinted at it to see what Gemma meant. She made such a comical face in doing it, that Gemma started giggling. That set Stacey off and the two of them were shouted at by their teacher, who put them on opposite sides of the class.

During mid-morning playtime, Jon got into a fight. Stacey couldn't believe it. Jon, who was normally so laid back and cheerful, had punched one of his classmates on the nose! He was made to stay in at lunchtime, so Stacey heard the story – or some of it – from his best buddy Ben. All Ben could say was that Jon had been arguing with Darren Sprike, when suddenly Jon had hit him in the face. It had made Darren's nose bleed, and Jon was in big trouble!

Stacey collected Jon from his classroom at the end of school. "What have you been doing Jon?" she asked, as she took his hand and walked down the driveway to the school gates. She was conscious that her hair had dried into a red frizz.

"I hit Darren Sprike," he replied, as if that was all anyone needed to know.

"Yeah, but *why*?"

"He said we hadn't got a mother, and I said, 'Yes we have,' and he said 'Where is she then?' and I said, 'I dunno,' and he said, 'She doesn't want you to know 'cos she hates you,' and when he said that, he poked his face right into mine – so I punched it."

"Oh Jon!" Stacey laughed – and squeezed his hand. "I think I'd have done the same!"

"Yes, you would," Jon replied, confidently.

Just outside the school gate, Darren Sprike stood

holding his mother's hand. They were obviously waiting for Stacey and Jonathan. Stacey's heart sank.

"You nasty bully! Look what you've done to my Darren!" Mrs Sprike yelled. Darren was holding his nose and had started crying loudly.

At the back of her mind, Stacey thought he sounded like wheezy old bagpipes. She glared at Mrs Sprike as she tried to get past, but Darren's Mum stood in front of them, and thrust her face into Stacey's – not aware of the volcanic temperament:

"Since your mother left, you Farr kids have become a couple of unruly little brats!"

Stacey blew her top. Her eyes blazed, and she bared her teeth in a way that took Mrs Sprike aback: "Not half as unruly as your precious Darren! Talking about brats are we? Well he's a *nasty, spiteful* brat! Ask *him* why Jonathan hit him! He deserved what he got!"

Jonathan was gaping at her – he knew Stacey's temper – but was scared that she'd lost it with the wrong person.

"I'm gonna tell my big brother of you," sneered Darren, forgetting that he was supposed to be crying, "and he'll come and beat you up!"

"Oh *will* he?" Stacey snarled, turning suddenly on Darren, who took a step backwards. "That's just the sort of thing I would expect from a little coward like you! I tell you what – it's a good job I wasn't around when you were hassling Jon – 'cos if I *had* been, you'd be holding more than your nose!" And with that, she dragged Jonathan past, stepping into the road as she did so.

A passing car narrowly missed them – its horn blasting – making them jump.

By the time they got home, they were both feeling pretty miserable. Matters were not improved when they discovered that dad was out. Stacey switched on the telly, made them a drink and got the biscuit tin. They sat and watched cartoons but neither of them seemed able to cheer up.

Finally, to their relief, dad came home. He had managed to get the car going, even though it had taken most of the day. "I got fish and chips!" he announced. "And a big carton of chocolate chip ice-cream!"

They all rushed around getting plates, cutlery, salt and vinegar and tomato sauce. Then, as they ate, they told dad what a disastrous day it had been. Dad was very thoughtful. "You should never hit people, Jonathan, unless it's to defend yourself."

"I *was* defending myself!"

"Hmm. Well, I understand why you did it, son. I might well have done the same thing myself..."

"Stacey would have hit him, she *said* she would!" Jonathan dipped an extra large chip into the blob of tomato sauce on his plate and crammed it into his mouth. "And you should have heard what she said to Darren's mum!"

Dad had got up to fill the kettle, and what with Jonathan's full mouth and the noise of the kettle filling, he didn't catch what Jonathan was saying. Stacey kicked him under the table and glared a warning at him. She didn't want dad to find out about her set-to with Mrs Sprike. Dad was putting out mugs, milk and sugar.

"What was that about Darren's mum?"

"He was just saying how horrible she was to us, when we came out of school this afternoon," Stacey replied, giving Jonathan another kick, to stop him from giggling.

Dad finally decided he would come to the school and talk to Jon's teacher, to see if he could try and set a few things straight. Jonathan wasn't sure if he wanted his dad to come to the school. But it was Friday evening and nothing much mattered for the next two days. He watched in happy expectation, as Stacey served out great dollops of chocolate ice-cream.

*

Later, when Jon was in bed and dad was at the computer doing his accounts, Stacey sauntered out into the garden. The usual lovely evening scents wafted over her. Everything was fresh after the rain. The clouds had cleared and the first few stars glimmered. She stood for a long time with her face lifted toward them. How far away they were. Were there people up there? Did they have problems? Did they suffer from heartache?

A voice from behind her made her jump. It was her dad. "You were far away – Stacey Farr..." he chuckled. "Where were you? Up there, with the aliens?"

"Yeah, I think I was dad. I just wondered – if they exist – whether they have problems like ours. I mean, are there alien schools which have sarcastic, horrible teachers? Do their schools have cruel kids in them, like Darren Sprike...?"

"Stacey..."

"Do alien mothers walk out on their families?" and quietly she began to cry.

"Stacey..." Dad put his arms round her and hugged her. He led her to the old wooden bench under the pear tree. "Mum... didn't exactly 'walk out' on us. The reason she went may surprise you." He laughed, but there was no sound of happiness in it. "I think it would surprise me!"

"Why would it surprise you? That's a daft thing to say dad!"

"Do you remember what work mum did?"

"Yes. She was a... a lab technician, wasn't she? At the research station in Ferndean." Stacey wiped her eyes on the back of her wrist.

"That's how she used to describe her work, but she was much more than that Stacey. She was one of their senior scientists." He smacked his forehead. "What am I saying... she *is* one of their senior scientists!"

"Was she? I mean... Is she? All I know is that she sometimes came home late and was very tired – but I thought that was just because they were busy." Stacey thought for a while, then said with a mixture of sadness and pride, "So mum was an important person then?" She smoothed her hair away from her face. "I wish I'd known. I'd have asked her all sorts of questions!"

"That was why she didn't let on what the true nature of her work was. Her boss, Professor... now what's his name? Fairchild! Professor Fairchild wanted their work to be kept secret, until they had some results to publicise. Before she left, they had made some kind of breakthrough in their research... she was very excited about it."

"What was it?"

"Well, you know the laboratory has to do with the science of arboriculture – the cultivation of trees and shrubs?"

"Er, yes..."

"In the spring of last year, a brilliant young scientist from New Zealand joined their team. In a few months, they thought they had finally cultivated the tree of their dreams. There were just a handful of saplings, but they had all the right characteristics."

Stacey was puzzled. "Right characteristics for what?"

"For planting and re-growing the tropical rain forests of course!"

"Why are they trying to cultivate tropical trees in England, for goodness sake?"

"Why not? Tropical conditions can be created in laboratories and greenhouses. Remember the Eden Project?"

"Oh yeah..." Stacey remembered their holiday in Cornwall last summer – and their visit to the vast plastic bubbles in an old quarry near the sea. "But what has all this got to do with mum leaving home?"

"We had a massive difference of opinion, which was never resolved." Dad sighed. "We fought about it for a week."

"Yes I think I remember that. It was awful. I could hear you arguing – so could Jon. Then you went round for days not talking to each other. I didn't say anything to Jon, but I thought she was... well... I thought she had fallen in love... with another man." Stacey began to cry again.

"It wasn't that at all, Stace." Dad sat remembering. All Stacey could see was his profile in the half-light. Then he carried on. "She wanted to take part in an experiment."

"What sort of experiment?"

"She was forbidden to tell me. It was classified – that

means top secret. But she said she might not live through it."

Stacey gasped. "But why did she want to do it, if it was that dangerous? Couldn't she tell you *anything* about it dad?"

"No she couldn't. All I knew was that it had to do with protecting the environment. And it meant that she had to go away."

"Go away where?"

"That was something else she couldn't tell me." Dad shook his head in frustration. "All I know is that the place itself was extremely dangerous."

"But if it was to protect the environment, how could it be so dangerous? Did she have to go and live in the jungle, or something?"

"I don't know... I don't know... she wouldn't say."

"Did you agree that she could go in the end?"

"Are you kidding? That was what the fight was about. I had this nightmare vision of mum going off and never coming back again!"

"So you told her she couldn't go." Stacey screwed her face up. "Dad, you know that would only make her more determined to go."

"Yes. But she genuinely felt that the trip itself was vital. We spoke about it almost all through the night before she was due to go. Without telling me too much, she wanted to impress upon me how significant it was. She cried a lot... said she didn't want to leave us... but that it meant so much... so much..." By this time his voice had become a whisper. "I think... that if something happened to her, she wanted to have told me as much as she possibly could. She wanted to be honest, without telling the truth – can you understand that?"

"I think so. But dad, mum's still alive, isn't she?" Then as her dad didn't answer straight away, she persisted anxiously. "*Isn't* she dad?"

"Oh yes. But where on earth she is Stace, I couldn't possibly tell you."

*

Stacey left her dad sitting on the bench and went to see how her seeds were doing. They wouldn't need watering because it had rained quite hard earlier. She was hoping that she might just see a tiny green shoot coming from one or two of them.

She got a shock. Where she had planted the seeds, there were eight little plants. The word 'beautiful' leapt into her mind. They were small, perfectly formed little shrubs, about fifteen centimetres tall, with glossy dark green leaves. She lay on the ground and peered at their stems, to make sure that they really did come from the seeds she had planted. They did – and as she brought her face up close she became aware of a heavenly perfume. She lay on the damp ground with her head on her folded arms, and breathed deeply. Peace...

Starting at the very roots of her hair, it seemed to ripple down the length of her body. She felt as though she were lying in a warm and gentle sea. Stacey smiled and sighed a deep, long sigh.

"Stacey! What are you doing?"

"Nothing much dad. Just relaxing."

"Well the ground's a bit wet for that, love. If you're tired you should go to bed."

Stacey sat up, still smiling. "Dad, when did I plant those seeds that Mr Bascombe sold me?"

"Last night.... Stace, you must be patient – you won't see anything yet!"

"Dad – look!"

Dad did look. "Those can't be what you planted last night!"

"Oh yes they are!" Stacey replied with a giggle, "Just have a sniff!"

Dad got down on all fours and breathed in the perfume of the plants."Wow! That's fantastic! You should be able to bottle it!" Dad started to laugh – and lay down on the grass. Stacey knew he was being flooded with peace. He wore a huge, daft grin.

Then he sat up. "They must have come from the tropics. I've never known anything grow that quick. They say stuff grows overnight in places like the Amazon. Your mum would probably know what they were. She'd have the Latin name for them and probably be able to tell you the exact forest they came from! I wonder where Bascombe got them?"

"Probably the Amazon!"

"To be honest with you Stace, I don't think he and Mrs Bascombe have been much further than Bognor!" Dad got to his feet and held a hand out to Stacey. "C'mon m'girl, it's way past your bed time, and if you're anything like me, you'll be shattered."

Dad locked and bolted the back door, while Stacey plodded up the stairs and went straight to bed without even bothering to wash or clean her teeth.

That night they both slept long and deep.

# Chapter Seven

**FABIAN**

It was just as well that the next day was Saturday. Jonathan always slept until he was woken up, and Stacey and her dad didn't wake up until ten o'clock. It was the telephone ringing that got the Farr household on the go. Dad thumped downstairs saying he couldn't believe how late it was. Stacey heard him on the phone, telling Gaynor-down-the-road that of course she could bring Fabian up in half an hour. Stacey would be glad to baby-sit him for the rest of the morning.

Stacey hated baby-sitting. Most of all, she hated baby-sitting Fabian. He was a big, fat, red-cheeked baby of about eighteen months. He nearly always seemed to be teething and was therefore nearly always crying, and nearly always had a runny nose. She only baby-sat Fabian because Gaynor-down-the-road paid her. She just had time to wash, dress and gobble down some sugar puffs, before Gaynor turned up.

"You are a good girl to do this for me at such short notice!" Gaynor beamed at Stacey when she opened the door. "There Fabe! It's your special friend, Stacey!"

Fabe did not think Stacey was a special friend, and immediately burst into tears.

Gaynor's face screwed up in exaggerated sympathy. "There there, darlin' – mummy'll only be gone for a little while. You just be a good boy and mummy'll bring you some sweeties!" She leant forward to hand Fabian over to Stacey, and as she did so, Fabian began to scream and sob and both little fat hands grabbed at strands of his mum's long hair. There followed a struggle to get Gaynor free from her oversized, clinging infant.

Stacey was furious with her dad. He should have asked her if she wanted to baby-sit! It was all right for him. He was in his workshop, making kitchen furniture for someone in the village. What if she'd had something else to do? What if she had wanted to go for a walk with a friend? She knew what her dad would have said, "Take Fabian with you!" She finally got him free of his mother – and Gaynor scuttled away quickly down the garden path. She was visiting the hairdresser, having told Stacey that she was going for a 'change of image'.

Stacey glared with loathing at the red, yelling blob sitting in the middle of the carpet. How on earth was she going to put up with, let alone care for, this impossible little human for a couple of hours? Jonathan came in, still in his pyjamas, with his box of Lego and dumped it down in front of Fabian. "There! Don't cry Fabian, you can play with this!" he said loudly, putting his face in front of the baby's. Fabian carried on bawling his head off and Jon shrugged at Stacey as if to say, "Well, I tried!"

"It's nice of you Jon, but I think it's a bit too old for him. There might be little pieces that he can put in his mouth and choke on."

Jonathan made a face and pulled the box away. "I

know, I'll go and see if dad has got any nice big chunks of wood."

"Yeah, then if he's teething, he can bite on those."

A few minutes later Jon came whizzing back inside. "Dad showed me your bushes Stacey! Wo! They're special! They smell great!"

He was carrying two nice smooth lumps of wood, the right size for Fabian to bite on, but too big for him to put right inside his mouth. He put them on the floor in front of the baby who was still crying noisily. Then he felt in his pocket and brought out a small, glossy leaf.

"What's that?" Stacey asked, suspiciously.

"It's off one of your bushes!" He held it under his nose and grinned.

"Jon, those are my plants! You're not to touch them!"

"It's only one leaf – there's loads more!"

Then, for no reason at all, he put the leaf on top of Fabian's head.

The screaming stopped like magic. He gazed up at the children with huge, tear-filled, blue eyes. They gazed back at him, then at each other. Stacey found some paper kitchen towel and gently dabbed his eyes. She wiped the red cheeks and the snotty nose, and as she did so, Fabian began to smile. Stacey didn't think she had ever seen Fabian smile. The smile transformed him. Fabian was actually a beautiful baby.

Beautiful!

# Chapter Eight

## HOME PLANET

Over the thousands of years, the people of Home Planet have consistently made the right decisions. They have never abused or polluted their globe. They have worked along with nature. Their technology is of the most advanced, but never have those advances been made at the expense of the environment.

Their people don't suffer from sickness the way Earth people do. Almost the only use they have for medicine is to assist with childbirth and to ease the aches and pains of old age. Of course, there are accidents and there is crime, (although compared with Earth, the rates are low) so injuries have to be dealt with. That is why in various locations stand the 'formularies'. For every circumstance in which medicine is required, healing leaves – in a variety of formulae – provide the needed cure.

So, as well as growing wild, the leaves are cultivated in crop fashion, and when they come into flower the wind carries their fragrance far and wide.

Fossil fuels like coal and oil are not used on Home Planet. Solar power, wind and wave power – any power source that is non-polluting serves their needs. Everything manufactured is from natural materials. When metals are required, these are extracted from mines that go only so deep, produce only so much. No resource is ever exhausted.

They are not meat eaters – although the forests and fields of Home teem with birds and animals, its lakes, rivers and seas swarm with fish. They farm the land in careful rotation. They waste neither the soil, nor what grows from it. They waste nothing. There is one world government and only one language. The inhabitants of Home live long and fulfilling lives. It is easy to see why, that in every way, Home Planet has advanced far ahead of Earth.

It was in a fairly recent exploration of their universal neighbourhood, that they discovered Earth. Its presence at first thrilled astronauts and scientists alike. Another beautiful planet – and it *was* beautiful. They relished the thought of inter-stellar travel, making friends across the light years. It was especially appealing that Earth dwellers are physically identical to Homefolk.

Then they found out the truth. Earth was sick. If they befriended its inhabitants, they too might become sick. Home scientists saw that over the thousands of years, Earth's inhabitants had made many wrong decisions. And the planet was dying. Home scientists thought at first that they might be able to give help to Earth by offering its superior technology. But they quickly dropped that idea when they realised that on Earth, people have a terrible habit of misusing whatever power comes within their reach. So Earth lay across the vast vacuum of space – and Home Planet scientists and astronauts marked its downward spiral.

In looking back, historians will never be able to pinpoint exactly what it was that changed the minds of the Home Planet government. It might have been Earth's News reports. Relayed by satellite from one part of Earth to another, Home technicians needed only to hack in to find out the latest. People watched as pictures of starving children, of raging wars and acts of terrorism, of massive earthquakes, freak weather conditions, strange and frightening sicknesses, man-made disasters such as plane and train crashes, flickered across the screens of Home monitors.

There was no doubt that with their superior resources, they could – and should – render assistance to Earth. But how could they do it without putting themselves in danger?

*

After much discussion, they eventually decided on a project that would involve sending a team of mental energists from Home Planet to Earth. Once there, using a globeringer shoe as a base, each energist would seek an Earth twin, a counterpart, someone with whom they could form a genuine friendship. The 'twinning' would depend entirely on minds that were alike, not on sameness of age or sex.

After the trust of an Earth twin had been won, it would only need a time of relaxation, maybe a time when he or she was sleeping, to perform a mind-lock. The mental energist would use this mental contact to pour into the twin's mind a dream... inspiration... the very seeds of an idea, which would be left to grow, just as an embryo develops in its mother's womb.

Dreams are so easily forgotten, but in this case they wouldn't be. On waking, the twin would feel refreshed, mentally stimulated. It had been more than a dream... it was more like a brainwave... he or she had seen a different future and it was beautiful. Beautiful! The dream would spark new ways of thinking. There would be excited talk, ideas and experiments. Its effects would become more and more productive as the results were put to use.

Project EarthAid was launched – and seemed to be working well. In various parts of Earth people were coming up with flashes of genius. News headlines began to appear in one country after another with words like 'New!', 'Amazing!', 'Revolutionary!', 'Bright Future!', and 'Wonder Drug!' Scientists, politicians, teachers, doctors, social workers, were presenting clever ways of dealing with the distressing problems of Earth.

Those monitoring progress back on Home Planet were pleased with the results of the project, but they were concerned that all this inspiration might attract the unwelcome attention of Intercept, the predatory Earth agency who made it their business to seek out and capture any form of extraterrestrial life.

Then, something happened which caused almost all energists to be recalled immediately.

# Chapter Nine

## RESEARCH AT FERNDEAN

Stacey's mum had worked in the laboratories at the Ferndean research station for six years. She and Stacey's dad had decided that because the work she did was so important, he would carry on his carpentry business from home, whilst she worked full time. That way, the children would always have someone to come home to after school – and mum would be able to give her undivided attention to her job.

Elizabeth Farr was part of a team whose research involved plant life – particularly trees. They were working to develop a strain of tree which would grow fast and strong and which could be planted by the thousands, to replace those lost because of the slashing and burning that was taking place in the tropical rain forests.

The laboratories had special greenhouses containing hundreds of samples. Labelled saplings grew out of pots and troughs in a special steamy atmosphere. A careful record was kept of how fast each one grew and a special note was made of those trees which grew fast but still stayed healthy and strong. They were making some progress but it was slow.

Then a new young scientist joined the team.

*

They welcomed his arrival. His name was Rob, and according to his references he had studied at a famous university in New Zealand. He got on well with everyone and settled very quickly into his job as junior scientist. He was a tremendous help to Elizabeth. Not only was he friendly and funny, but he worked very hard.

She would arrive at the lab some mornings and find that Rob had prepared everything for the experiment he knew they would be conducting that morning. He had an instinct for directing their research in a way that achieved results. Rob and Elizabeth often sat in the canteen and talked about work all through the lunch hour – and then they'd laugh at themselves for not having had a change of subject.

She had tried a few times to invite Rob back home to Hollybrook, to meet the family and have tea with them, but he always seemed to be too busy. One day, some months after he had come to Ferndean, he came to tell her that there was an emergency at home and that he would be flying back to New Zealand within the next few days.

He was not too sure if he would be back. It was a shame. Elizabeth knew that Stacey and Jonathan would have liked him. She had told them all about him, and now they would never meet him! On his last day, she gave him a good telling off for leaving. At the same time though, she gave him a gift – wooden bookends carved by Peter, to take home with him.

They were sitting in the rest room after having lunched together in the canteen. Elizabeth felt depressed that they were losing such a valuable work mate. "Write to us," she told him, handing him their address and phone number on a card. "And if you're ever in England again, get in touch and we'll put you up!"

"Thanks Liz – you've been a good friend. Give my regards to that family of yours!"

"I will. I wish you hadn't been too busy to meet them!" She put her head back and closed her eyes.

"Suddenly, I feel tired." She yawned. "Don't worry though, I'm not about to fall asleep!"

But she did.

*

At first the dream trickled into her subconscious like a colourful stream. Then it grew in volume until it was a bright cascade. She saw a scarred landscape, a road slashed through a mutilated forest, fires burning out of control, animals, birds, insects, homeless – or dead. But as she watched, trees began to grow from the ruined landscape. They grew before her very eyes – strong and healthy, rich and green. They took command. The fires went out under the onslaught of such growth. Animals took refuge in the advancing forest; birds flocked to their branches. "Home! Home!" they seemed to be calling to each other in excitement.

Then the dream trees turned to her. There was something important they wanted to tell her... something that would benefit the work she was doing. As they got closer to her, she became aware of a heavenly perfume... she breathed deeply... peace flooded through her... it was beautiful!

It was as the trees leaned close to give away their precious secret that something very strange happened. She glanced up through their leafy branches and beheld a night sky full of stars and planets. She found her gaze riveted on one planet in particular – and as she looked – it grew, until it filled her vision. It was a blue and green planet just like Earth, but it wasn't Earth. She could see the oceans and the land masses. She could make out the mountain ranges. And over and around the planet, draped like a delicate shawl, were – clouds. "Home! Home!" She could hear the echo of the bird calls.

She awoke suddenly to find Rob staring at her. There was something so intense in his gaze that, in spite of knowing him well, she became slightly afraid.

"Where are you *really* from?" Elizabeth demanded.

# Chapter Ten

## DOWNLOADING THE DREAM

The mental energists were experiencing difficulties. True, they had made some headway – but a few of their subjects were waking up before they had finished downloading the dream. Why?

An Earth studies expert came up with the answer – and it was simple. On Earth, adults were not good dreamers. They had become worldly wise. They were weary and sceptical. Some of them still had dreams and could expand their minds to take in new ideas. But the attitudes and approach to life of so many of them had hardened. The expert suggested a way round the problem that, to begin with, was not well received.

"*Children* would respond much better," he told them. "Children are impressionable. Their minds are still wide open. They would respond eagerly to the dreams we have to give them. Once their imaginations are fired, they can change the course their education will take – and so change Earth history!

True, the progress towards a better Earth will be that much slower. Children will have to grow up before they can have any influence – and make a difference. But bright ideas will come much more naturally from a new generation. Also – and this is very important – we are less likely to arouse the suspicions of Intercept, because of there being a sudden Earth-wide rush of brainwaves."

However... " and here, the Earth studies expert gazed anxiously around the Committee Chamber, "there is a major problem. We cannot send *adult* energists down to befriend Earth children."

The EarthAid Committee listened respectfully, but they had a feeling that they weren't going to like what was coming.

"So, my fellow scientists, we must send our children."

There was a deathly hush. *Send their precious children to such a dirty, dangerous planet?* No way!

On Home Planet though, probably because they enjoy such good health and they live such long lives, they don't make hasty decisions. They have lengthy, careful discussions. There are no loud, bitter arguments. All the 'ifs' and 'buts' are sifted through and sorted out. So finally they agreed. Children – specially chosen children, supervised children – could successfully make the trip.

These junior energists would be trained – just as the adults had been – to seek an Earth twin. Not necessarily someone of the same age or sex – but someone of like mind. Even so, they would be encouraged to look for those with imagination – the sensitive ones, the dreamers. Those who, in spite of sometimes being laughed at or bullied, hung onto their dreams.

Once the twin had been found – and trust had been established – a mind-lock would be relatively easy. The beauty of it was, being children, they could make a game of it. Pretending to read one another's minds, or just closing their eyes and describing their daydreams. During such an easy, light-hearted moment, the mind-lock could take place and the special dream downloaded.

Of course, the very nature of children would bring its own risks. Because of their natural, uninhibited behaviour, children would be prone to leave traces. The only thing their instructors could do, was to remind them again and again – to be very careful.

## Chapter Eleven

### RE-MASK

The same rain that soaked Stacey on the way to school on Friday morning, woke Mab as it drummed on the roof of the shoe. She checked the time and was surprised to see it was so late. By this time, Ean should surely have re-masked the shoe and been on the road again.

Globeringer shoes were invented to become as big as was necessary for their passengers' needs. So just now, the shoe was the size of a small bedroom. Mab looked over to where Ean was sleeping – and got a terrible shock. Ean was quite obviously ill. She was asleep, but her cheeks were bright red and her breathing was noisy. Mab had never met anyone sick before. Hardly anyone at Home got sick. She had seen reports from Earth though and recognised the signs.

"What's wrong?" Brod was sitting up in his sleep-chair, his hair standing on end. Normally Mab would have laughed – he looked so funny – but now she stared at him and mouthed the words, "Ean – is – sick!"

"Sick?" repeated Brod. "She can't be sick... how could she be?"

"I don't know! We were all immunised against Earth sicknesses, weren't we?"

"Yes. You must be wrong, Mab!" He moved across to Ean's sleep-chair and touched her face with the back of his hand. But he withdrew his hand sharply and took a step backward. "She *is* sick!" he exclaimed in horror.

"Of course she is – stupid! The thing is, how did she *get* sick? And..." Mab bit her lip and felt tears come to her eyes, "is she going to die?"

"Of course she isn't going to die!" Brod snapped. But he was staring at Ean with fear in his eyes.

By this time the other two had woken up. Mab told them of Ean's sickness and they reacted the same way as she and Brod had.

"How did she get sick?" asked Treo.

"It could have been that policeman she was talking to." Jay sounded as though he knew a thing or two about it. "He might have been the disease carrier. But then most Earth people are."

"I really don't like this planet!" Treo muttered.

"The thing is, what shall we do?" Brod asked. "We have to carry on somehow, but without Ean in charge it's going to be difficult. Can we make her better?"

"We should contact watch captain on the far-reacher," Jay said.

This sounded like such good sense that they all breathed a sigh of relief. Mab stood in front of the console and prepared to send a message. But just then, they heard voices outside the shoe.

*

"Who the devil put this here, Watson? How long has it been up?"

61

"I dunno Mr Russell, sir.... it wasn't here yesterday!"

"This hay is not from my fields. I didn't grow hay this year, as you know!"

"I dunno where it came from Mr Russell, sir. It wasn't here yesterday!"

"Stop repeating yourself man! Find out who put it here! Better still, load it onto a trailer – we can use it for animal feed."

Inside the shoe the children, with their newly-learned English, stared at each other in alarm. What now? It wouldn't take much prodding to convince the men that this was no ordinary haystack, in fact not really a haystack at all! Mab, with shaky fingers, lifted the cover on the emergency pad and touched it gently. This gave the shoe direct access to watch captain.

"Globeringer Five – what is your request?" came a comforting voice through the receiver. Mab spoke quickly, trying to keep the panic out of her voice.

"Watch captain, we badly need help. Ean, our group leader is sick. At the moment we are a haystack in a field somewhere in the countryside. It was our plan to re- mask and go on, but someone has discovered us and is talking about pulling the haystack apart!"

"Who is speaking, G5?"

"I am Mab. The others are Brod, Treo and Jay. Can you help us watch captain?"

"Sit tight down there Mab. Fasten yourselves in – including your group leader – and stand away from the control panel."

The children brought their sleep-chairs – and Ean's – to an upright position and made themselves secure. Lights on the console began to flicker, as from somewhere outside the Earth's atmosphere, the far-reacher began to re-mask the shoe by remote control.

Out in the field, Watson, who had returned with a tractor and trailer, looked on in disbelief as the offending haystack began to glow with rainbow colours – changing, almost melting, until it took on the shape of what was most definitely.... a Land Rover.

Watson, paralysed with fright, drove the tractor straight into a ditch at the side of the field. Perhaps it was for the best that he was found unconscious. When he woke up in hospital sometime towards evening, no-one believed his story of a shape-shifting haystack. They all humoured him gently – and put it down to severe concussion.

But Watson's story was overheard by a reporter, who was in the hospital investigating a food poisoning scare. He didn't believe it either, but he thought it would fill a column or two in the local Gazette. He visualised the headline: "Farm Worker Blames Accident On Shape-Shifting Haystack." Watson, of course, was only too happy to talk about it.

*

The children voted Jay to drive the shoe. He was easily the tallest of the group, and might just pass as an adult to any curious, passing motorists. They decided to put a good distance between them and the field they had just left, perhaps finding some secluded woodland where they might park without being discovered.

They kept to the quietest roads they could find in case anyone seeing them re-mask had raised the alarm. The area south of them was mapped out in detail on one of the screens and Treo keyed in the required destination, knowing that MAD would highlight the most straightforward route to their planned destination.

Unfortunately this did not help Jay in dealing with the peculiarities of the traffic system. He kept to the left as he had seen Ean do, but he was unnerved by the various signs and signals.

"What do I do here?" he asked, as they approached a set of traffic lights.

Treo was desperately trying to speed-swot the English Highway Code from MAD's Earth manual. "Okay. If there's a green light, you drive straight through them – " Treo glanced up. The lights were green. "If there's an amber light, prepare to stop. If there's a red light, stop." She looked up again. "Jay – if there's a red light, stop. Jay, *Jay – STOP!*" Jay, giving a sudden shriek, brought the shoe to a jerking stop.

"What is the matter with you?" demanded Mab. "Aren't you listening to Treo's instructions?"

"I'm so sorry Mab," Jay said sweetly over his shoulder, as a stream of cars and trucks passed crossways in front of them, "but you should try driving one of these for the first time, under stressful circumstances, on a wet, slippery road..." His voice got louder until he was almost shouting."...on an *ALIEN PLANET!!*" He turned and glared at her. "Now are you going to let me drive, or would you like to take over?"

Mab didn't answer but Treo sang out, "Lights are green. Go!"

Jay whipped round to the controls and the vehicle jumped forward, jerking everyone back in their seats.

Nobody dared say anything. Mab quickly checked on Ean and was relieved to find her still asleep.

Somewhere along the route to Hollybrook, the children were seeking refuge.

"There's an unclassified road branching off into woodland. It's a right turn, about a mile on." Treo had her finger on the screen map.

"I'll watch out for it," Jay replied.

Happily, when Jay – without signalling – made a sudden lurching turn to the right, there were no other vehicles in sight. They bumped up the rough track and parked deep inside the wood. The doors were opened and the children breathed in rain-washed air. Jay left the driver's seat and came over to Ean. He lengthened her sleep-chair and felt her forehead with the back of his hand.

"Poor Ean," he muttered, looking as helpless as he felt. Rather than do nothing, he brought cool water and began to sponge her face. Privately, he wished they carried a supply of healing leaves – but then no-one was expecting to fall ill.

Treo was making drinks for everyone. Brod and Mab prepared food. Slowly, subtly, the shoe expanded to accommodate its busy passengers. On the outside though, it was still just an ordinary, well used Land Rover.

Mab joined Brod, who was sitting on the Land Rover step sampling the food they had prepared. "What can we do to help Ean?" she sighed. "We haven't a clue how to cure Earth sicknesses. We don't even know what's wrong with her."

"I think it's what they call flu," he replied. "I saw a documentary on it once. It's a virus, very common on

Earth. Some strains can be dangerous – fatal even. I'm not sure how it would affect people from Home though…"

"When she wakes up, we must make sure that she gets plenty to drink. We should also call the far-reacher again. Watch captain will know what we should do next. We can't very well go on without a group leader."

Brod chewed thoughtfully for a while then he said, "Of course, if we had some healing leaves it would make all the difference, but they don't grow on this miserable planet."

Mab, who had been chewing, stopped. Then she gulped before she had finished her mouthful and started to choke. Brod thumped her on the back until she could breathe properly again. "Steady on Mab – are you all right?"

"Yes thanks." She took a few good deep breaths to make sure. Then, as if she had made up her mind about something, she added solemnly, "Brod, there is something I think I must tell you…"

# Chapter Twelve

## COMING CLEAN

"*WHAT?!!*"

They had walked a short distance from the shoe and were standing under some dripping trees.

"I can't believe you brought seeds to this planet, Mab... after all the warnings about not bringing anything!"

Mab hung her head. She liked Brod – and this was awful! At the same time though, she was hugely relieved to have told someone. She peered at him whilst not moving her head. He was shocked, scared, but he also looked awestruck with her. *She had broken the rules!*

"Why didn't you say something to Ean about having the seeds in your pocket? You put us all in terrible danger. What if we're traced?"

"You think I haven't thought of that?" Mab replied quietly. "But I was thinking about how much our visit meant to the Earth – and what would happen if we had to suddenly abort the mission. It would be such a waste of great ideas and dreams." And she added even more quietly, "Genno said it would be devastating – and it would be."

There was a long silence. Rain pattered on the leaves above. Occasionally a gust of wind would blow, making them both feel the cold. Mab began to feel very depressed. The excitement of the trip had driven thoughts of home and family out of her mind but now she longed to be back with them all. She thought of Bo's funny face – and his deep chuckle. She pictured her mum and dad, so proud of her, trying to hide their anxiety as they waved her goodbye. Proud of her. They were PROUD OF HER!

They wouldn't be proud of this wet, gloomy female. Then a thought skipped out of Brod's mind into hers: *"Let's get them back!"* – and she looked up startled.

There is a rule of politeness on Home Planet – where mind reading is perfectly normal. You never read anybody's mind unless that person is related to you, or is a close friend of long standing. To read the mind of someone you don't know very well is the height of bad manners. Also, it is considered very rude to project your thoughts into the mind of a stranger, or someone you have only recently met. Although the children had been through training together and were now team-mates, they hadn't yet reached that point of mental closeness – until now.

Strangely though, under the circumstances, she found it very comforting that in spite of being shy, Brod had made the first move to be on thinking-terms. Without looking up she projected back at him, *"Get what back?"*

*"The seeds, what d'you **think!**"*

*"How can we get them back? I told you what I did with them!"*

*"I remember the name and address on the side of the van."* Brod looked smug. *"Let's go and find Mr Bascombe!"*

*"You really think we can track down a small handful*

*of seeds? They've probably fallen down the back of the seat, or onto the floor – or even out onto the road!"* She paused just for a moment then, her eyes gleaming: *"But I reckon it's worth a try!"*

When they returned to the shoe, they saw that Ean had woken up and was sipping water. She looked awful. She complained of a headache and a very sore throat, in a croaky voice that the children could hardly hear. She tried to apologise, but they wouldn't let her. They turned up the cool air system, gave her an extra pillow and asked if there was anything else she would like them to do for her.

"You'd better call watch captain... tell him of our latest problem..." she whispered. "I'd do it myself, but I don't think he would hear me!"

"They already know you're sick. We contacted the far-reacher this morning," said Jay.

"What did they tell you to do?" asked Ean.

Mab answered, "We thought watch captain would be shocked. But he just calmly gave us orders to fasten up and sit tight – then he re-masked us by remote control."

"Oh yes? What are we masked as?"

"We are a..." Treo screwed her face up trying to re-member its name, "...a Land Rover. It's one of those ve-hicles that can drive over rough ground as well as on the road systems."

"Sounds just the job to me." Ean sank back on her pillow with a groan and closed her eyes. The children gazed at each other with alarm. Ean smiled weakly. "Just let me sleep. I'll be all right. Call watch captain again."

The watch captain had changed shifts – a feminine voice came through the receiver. "Globeringer Europe

Five, we know you have problems down there. It's a little risky, but we want you to lie low for a day to give your group leader a chance to recover, which we think she will. We are almost certain that she is suffering from journey fatigue. If you feel you are in any danger though, you should re-mask and drive to a new location."

They listened carefully as watch captain reminded them how to speed-learn, telling them each to put earphones on – and plug into the central console. Mab activated a tiny screen, and locating the complete set of instructions for operating the shoe, she clicked on 'SPILL'.

In two minutes the children had learned not only how to drive the shoe, but to sail it and fly it. They learned how to mask and re-mask How to prepare for lift-off when it came to actually leaving Earth's surface, and how to use all its useful extras – including its defence systems.

They were told to rest for a few minutes, then the British Highway Code was downloaded. Jay was grinning as he realised what he was speed-learning. No more mishaps!

# Chapter Thirteen

## HOLLYBROOK

It was all very well for watch captain to say that Ean was suffering from 'journey fatigue', but the more the children studied Ean, the more uneasy they became. If she was simply over-tired, she would be weary and lifeless, or maybe she would keep falling asleep. But she had a high temperature, and when she dropped off to sleep, they were finding it difficult to wake her.

*"Mab. We need to find those seeds."* Brod popped a thought into her mind. *"If we found just one and planted it, it would grow in a few hours, and the leaves would make Ean well in no time."*

*"I agree. But there are two things to consider. One, the far-reacher has a lock on us, and although it wouldn't stop us moving away from here, they might want to know why we're going so soon. Two, we will have to tell Treo and Jay."*

*"I still think we should go, don't you? And we should tell Treo and Jay..."*

*"OK let's do it."*

\*

"*WHAT?!!*"

Jay gawped at Mab. "You're joking right?" He stared for a long time at Mab, then said, accepting with difficulty, "You're not joking."

"I'm not joking Jay. All I can say is, I'm so sorry. I completely forgot that I had the seeds in my pocket. I promise you I would never have knowingly brought them down to Earth..."

Treo broke in: "But you did bring them Mab, and although the thought of it is frightening, I think we should stop talking about it and go and find them. Where did you say you dropped them?"

"I was going to throw them away in a litter bin at the petrol station, but we were called back to the shoe, so I dropped them inside a van, onto the driver's seat – the driver had left the door open."

Jay stared at her. Then with a resigned expression, he took her face in his hands and pretended to head-butt her.

Mab didn't react.

"So it's just a matter of finding the van, wherever in the world it's gone," Jay observed sarcastically, "and breaking into it. Just where d'you suggest we start?"

"I remember the name and address that was on the side of the van, Jay."

"So it's not impossible to go and find the van, you see," Mab added quickly, "and breaking into it shouldn't be too difficult."

"But will the seeds still be there?" Treo sounded doubtful.

"We can only go and find out," said Mab.

They decided to re-mask – now they had learnt how

to. A new image would make it more difficult for anyone to trace them. Brod informed MAD that they wanted something not too flashy, and that they didn't want passing drivers to be able to see inside too well as none of the children, not even Jay really, looked old enough to drive.

A little later, a dark red people carrier with tinted windows turned out of a country lane and onto the main road. With the help of the on-screen map, they were heading for a village called Hollybrook, and a shop called Bascombes – which would have, they hoped, a small van parked outside.

*

They arrived in Hollybrook without further mishap. The vehicle – with Jay at the controls – was driving down the High Street and approaching a school. Groups of children chatted and laughed as they walked down the driveway to the school gate. They were obviously finishing for the day.

"Take care here Jay," warned Mab. "Slow right down. They have loads of accidents outside schools. We mustn't have an accident!" Jay slowed right down, but even as he did, a girl and a small boy, holding hands, stepped off the pavement right in front of them. He swerved to avoid them and blasted the horn. In the rear view mirror he saw the girl – with bright red hair – glaring after them. "Oops!" he said.

Further down on the left, they drove past Bascombes hardware store – and to their delight, the van was parked outside. They all gave a cheer.

"We need to park somewhere," Brod said.

"Yes, somewhere quiet, where perhaps we can't be seen." Treo was peering out of the side window as they passed on through the village. "What about up there?"

They were leaving Hollybrook behind and coming into countryside again, but they spied a narrow track leading to an old barn, which appeared deserted. Jay turned off, driving up the track and round the back of the barn. He stopped the engine and there was quiet. "How's Ean?" he asked.

Ean was not doing very well. The flush had gone from her cheeks and she was very pale. Her breathing was shallow.

Mab's spirits sank. "Right," she said briskly, trying to mask her fear. "Two of us should stay with Ean – and two of us should go into the village to try and get into that van."

"How *are* we going to get into that van? Ideas anyone?" Jay glanced at each of them in turn, then suggested, "Perhaps we could go in and ask the guy if he would mind us ransacking his shop, because we're from an alien planet and seem to have mislaid some seeds that one of us rather stupidly brought with us..." He was treated to three withering stares.

There was a short silence as they racked their brains, then Brod said, "We could pretend we were trying to earn some money – and offer to clean the van."

"Or one of us could actually go into the shop and ask them if they have any seeds," Mab added, slightly desperate.

"By the way, what is a hardware store?" Treo wanted to know. "What do they sell?"

"Well, when we passed, I noticed buckets and brooms and gardening tools outside," Jay offered.

"Gardening tools?" Mab suddenly brightened. "Then they might have seeds too!"

"Mab, you're not expecting to find your eight little healing seeds among all the others, are you?"

Mab smiled mysteriously.

## Chapter Fourteen

### BASCOMBES

Because Brod had come up with the suggestion of cleaning Mr Bascombe's van, he was told by the others that he could go and do it! And because the seeds had belonged to Mab, she went with him. They decided they should not be away for longer than an hour. Jay and Treo agreed to stay with Ean.

Mr Bascombe was the first human Brod had spoken with on a one-to-one basis, and he wasn't enjoying the experience.

"WHAT CAN I DO FOR YOU, YOUNG MAN?" he bawled across the counter, as Brod strolled in.

"I wondered if you needed your van washing – sir..." said Brod, unaware that Mr Bascombe was deaf.

"YOU'LL 'AVE TO SPEAK UP!" Brod approached the counter and repeated his offer in a much louder voice.

"NO, NO, NO, YOUNG MAN. MY GRANDSON WASHES MY CAR – AND MY VAN – ON SATURDAY MORNINGS. YOUNG STEPHEN MAKES A SMASHING JOB OF IT – WASHES IT TIL IT SPARKLES!"

It was unfortunate that this reply had a lot of 'S' sounds in it, because every time Mr Bascombe said 'S', Brod received a liberal spraying. It was all he could do to prevent himself from diving for cover on his side of the counter. He backed away one or two steps and remembering to speak very loudly, he said he hoped he didn't mind his asking.

"NOT AT ALL, YOUNG MAN. COME TO THINK OF IT, I'VE NOT SEEN YOU BEFORE, HAVE I? ARE YOU NEW AROUND HERE?"

"I'm just visiting," answered Brod, taking another step back, to make sure he was out of range.

"OH YES? YOU GOT RELATIVES HERE THEN?" Mr Bascombe persisted.

"Er, just visiting friends, really."

"FRIENDS – WHO MIGHT THEY BE THEN? I KNOW EVERYONE HEREABOUTS!" At the end of 'hereabouts' a small blob of spit actually got as far as Brod's nose. As he wiped it off with his sleeve he was wondering how to answer Mr Bascombe's question. He was glad when the shop door opened and someone walked in.

"Oh it's you Mab." He couldn't keep the relief out of his voice. Mab grinned at him and said 'Hi' – but she was bombarding his mind with her thoughts: *"Keep him talking Brod, ask him what he's got in the way of seeds. I'm going to pretend to look at some stuff on his shelves while I read his mind!"*

*"Good idea, but hurry up, this human shouts – and spits!"* Brod became aware of the giggle taking shape in Mab's mind.

*"It's not funny Mab – it's disgusting!"* But Mab, trying hard not to laugh, had moved into a corner and was pretending to study the fertilizers.

"This is my sister," Brod shouted, jerking his head in Mab's direction.

"OH YES, INTERESTED IN GARDENING IS SHE?"

Brod was glad Mr Bascombe didn't hear the sudden explosion of mirth in the corner. He raised his voice.

"Well, we both are – we've got a very big garden at home. What sort of seed selection do you have?"

Mr Bascombe indicated a revolving display with dozens of packets of seeds hanging on hooks. Brod became very interested. He picked up a packet and pretended to read the information on the back.

"YOU'RE LOOKING AT CELERY SEEDS, YOUNG MAN – DIFFICULT TO GROW SUCCESSFULLY."

Brod was glad to be well away from all those S's. "It does take a lot of effort, it's true," Brod yelled back. "But if you prepare your trenches and remember to earth the stems up at regular intervals – so that only the green leafy tips are showing – you'll get a good, long, crunchy stalk that isn't too stringy. Of course, you need a humus rich soil, and regular watering and feeding."

Mr Bascombe was astonished. How could he know that, to an inhabitant of Home Planet, gardening is second nature? His opinion of this strange young man rose a good few notches. He took a deep breath. "TELL ME, YOUNG MAN, DO YOU GROW TOMATOES?"

Brod thought of the wonderful, sweet, juicy tomatoes that grew on Home Planet, the size of large oranges. Then at the top of his voice he replied, "Yes I do, actually. I grow them in raised beds. I don't know about you, but I like to prepare the soil in winter – perhaps dig in some peat and a small amount of compost or manure." And to Mab he projected: *"For goodness sake be quick – I'm running out of voice!"*

"WHAT D'YOU DO ABOUT SOIL PESTS AND ROOT DISEASES?" More spit.

Brod went on at full volume, to give some tips that he thought would be useful for growing healthy tomatoes. It was fairly routine stuff but Mr Bascombe was impressed, so Brod asked, "My sister and I like to experiment. Do you ever get unusual seeds?"

"Not really... I sometimes get tropical flower seeds..." He thought for a moment, and unnoticed by him, Mab lifted her head with a little smile.

"TELL YOU WHAT THOUGH, YESTERDAY – NOW THAT WAS A DAY AND A HALF! YESTERDAY, I FOUND SOME WEIRD SEEDS IN MY CAR. DUNNO HOW THEY GOT THERE, BUT I PICKED 'EM UP AND... NOW WHERE DID I PUT 'EM?" He walked over to a small plastic tray on a shelf near the door. Then he stopped and exclaimed, "AH! I KNOW WHAT I DID WITH 'EM! I SOLD 'EM TO YOUNG STACEY FARR. SHE'S A KEEN GARDENER LIKE YOU. I JUST HAD A FEW ODD SEEDS LEFT OVER – AND I HAD 'EM ALL IN HERE!" He jiggled the empty tray.

The words 'Stacey' and 'seeds' produced two small spit bombs, and Brod thought it was high time he was going. "Well, never mind. I hope Stacey – who did you say...?"

"FARR – LIVES IN MULBERRY LANE..."

"I hope Stacey Farr makes good use of them. We really ought to be going now. Nice, er, talking to you."

"And you young man, young lady, call again... don't often get kids with such good sense..."

But Mab and Brod had gone.

# Chapter Fifteen

## MAX AND BRUTUS

They were tempted to go straight round to Mulberry Lane. Mab knew the house. She'd seen it in Mr Bascombe's mind, a white fence with a gate leading to a long front path – and on the front door, number eight! She had also got a clear picture of Stacey's face as the man had told Brod about giving her the seeds. However, they had promised not to be longer than an hour, and they had already taken three quarters. So they decided to report straight back to the shoe, letting them know that the search was nearly over.

"I didn't ask him when he gave Stacey the seeds," said Brod, as they walked down Hollybrook High Street.

"It was yesterday afternoon. When he said he'd had 'a day and a half' yesterday, his mind came alive with pictures of that petrol station. Then I could see him remembering how he found the seeds on the seat of his car – he'd been sitting on them of course. He simply scooped them up, took them inside the shop – and dropped them in that plastic tray, which already had a few other seeds in it. Stacey came in with a small boy. I saw that in his mind too, so it was probably after school."

"Mab, you're a genius!"

"Well for goodness sake! We're trained mental energists! With all the worry I forgot how easy it is to read the minds of Earth people!"

"So we just need to tell the others, then we can go back into the village and find Stacey's house."

As they walked down the village street, they gazed about them with open curiosity, aware that this was the first proper chance they'd had to take note of the everyday things of Planet Earth.

Just then, something small and furry shot through a gap in the hedge a few yards ahead of them and scampered away down the road. Behind the hedge lay the garden of an old flint cottage, and running down the path – a toddler tucked under her arm – came a young woman.

"Max!" she called. "Max! Come back here – you bad dog!"

To Brod and Mab, who didn't know there was such a thing as a *bad* dog, this was a fascinating turn of events. They watched the animal as it sped off into the distance – and Brod turned back to grin at the woman as she came through the gate. She was hot and flustered.

"He can certainly run fast!" he observed, trying to be friendly.

"Of course he can – he doesn't want to be caught!" The woman snapped at him, putting the toddler down, and holding its hand said, "You might at least have tried to stop him!"

"I'm sorry!" Brod exclaimed, remembering in an instant how humans liked to keep pets in a kind of domestic captivity. "Do you want me to get him back for you?"

"How can you?" the woman said, looking suspiciously near to tears. "He's probably miles away by now."

Unable to help himself, Brod began to use his alien skills. He narrowed his eyes. "He's actually still quite near! He's sniffing round somebody's back garden – I think they're having food out there, or something..."

"A barbecue probably – but how do you know?"

At this point Mab entered the conversation: "He's got a really keen sense of smell!" She nodded and smiled at the woman and at the same time trod on Brod's foot. *"Be careful!"* she thought to him.

But Brod was in his element with animals and brushed her warning aside. He set off down the High Street, giving a strange, high-pitched whistle. A few moments later, Max came out of a front gate and began to trot happily towards him, an uncooked beefburger hanging from the side of his mouth.

Brod crouched down and scooping the little dog up in his arms, removed the beefburger, tossing it aside with an expression of disgust. He began speaking softly in the Home tongue. The puppy whimpered in return as if to say, "You have no idea, the problems I have!" In fact that's more or less what he was saying, but only Brod understood.

He brought the dog back to its owner and set it down at her feet, saying, "He's frightened of the other dog, the big old fellow who sleeps in the room at the back of the house. He also doesn't like your little girl pulling his ears!" He glanced down at the toddler who hid behind her mother's legs.

"How do you know we have another dog?" The woman was mildly suspicious.

Mab was pouring alarms into Brod's mind: *"What are you doing, you idiot! Why don't you just tell her we're from another planet? She's going to find out pretty soon if you carry on like this!"*

She replied brightly – once more in Brod's behalf: "Oh, I think we must have seen it around, sometime or other!"

"May I see your other dog please?" asked Brod, and Mab groaned out loud even as her shoulders slumped.

"Sure!" the woman led the way down the garden path, deeply impressed by this youngster's talent with animals. "I'm afraid the house is in a bit of a mess..."

They entered an untidy front room, passing through it to a room at the back of the house. An old, black Labrador, who had been sleeping in a basket by the back door, rose to its feet, growling. Brod said something, and reassured, it tottered forward to meet him. Whilst the puppy hung back afraid, Brod crouched once more and took the old dog's face between his hands – whispering strange words to it.

"What language is that he's speaking?" the woman – whose name they discovered was Sue – asked Mab. Once more, Mab searched frantically through her mental database for a suitable answer. "Oh *that!"* she laughed, glaring at Brod. "His mother is from Scandinavia..."

Brutus – the old dog – returned peacefully to his basket. Brod said a few words to Max and he too curled up in the basket, inside the circle of Brutus' body. The old dog gave the puppy's face a couple of casual licks, then lay his face on the side of the basket with a gusty sigh. Lying there together, the two animals might always have been the best of friends.

Sue was amazed. She turned to Mab once more. "Er... which part of Scandinavia...?"

Once they had left the cottage, Mab walked several paces ahead of Brod. She was furious with him. And Brod, reading her thoughts, knew it.

To their dismay, when they got back to the old barn, the shoe was gone.

## Chapter Sixteen

**SNOOPER**

They just stood, looking stupidly at the space where it had been parked.

"Brod... where's it gone?"

Brod swallowed. "I don't know. Maybe they're inside the barn. C'mon!"

The huge barn doors had been hanging open, possibly for years. Brod and Mab crept into the gloom. A hulking old combine harvester took up most of the space. They found a rusty, upturned wheelbarrow and sat down, trying not to panic. What would cause Jay and Treo to move on without them? There must be some danger threatening. Had Intercept traced their whereabouts? They spoke in hushed whispers. Suddenly, there came to their ears a creaking noise, as if a door were opening slowly on rusty hinges. The two sat very still, their eyes wide with fright. From the rear of the combine harvester a voice reached them. "Mab, Brod – is that you?"

Whilst Mab and Brod had been at Bascombes, Treo and Jay had spotted a car parked on the verge a little way up the road. It didn't alarm them to begin with. People stop and park for any number of reasons. Then Jay saw that the driver, who was on his own, had taken out a pair of binoculars and was studying the barn. From that angle, the driver could see behind it, and was making no secret of the fact that he was interested in the people carrier.

The children had been playing a game out in the open, and just carried on as though they had every right to be there. After a while the car drove away, but they were thoroughly spooked, and decided to drive the people carrier inside the barn and re-mask. MAD had come up with a great disguise. What else would you expect to find inside an old barn, but a large, equally old piece of farm machinery? However, they felt far from safe.

"How's Ean?" asked Mab, after she and Brod had revealed the whereabouts of the seeds.

Treo stopped biting her nails to say, "About the same. She woke up for a short spell and had a drink, but she's sleeping again. I wouldn't mind, but she has a cough and it sounds as though she's having difficulty breathing!"

Jay said, "Could you two return to the village after dark?"

"Have we any idea of how we are going to get Stacey to give us the seeds?" Brod asked.

"That's if she hasn't planted them already. She might have planted them as soon as she got home yesterday." Jay's comment made them all think.

"We could sneak into her garden – we would know straight away, wouldn't we? Because of the perfume!"

But as Mab and Brod were about to set off after dark, they saw a car parked in the same place as before. They had only just tip-toed out – there was a bright moon – when the sight of it made them shrink quickly back into the shadows. Jay, using the night-viewer, confirmed that it was the same car.

"Is he looking at us?" Treo was chewing her nails again.

"Not at the moment – but why has he come again?"

"I don't know," said Brod "but we can't go out while he's there."

They had been peering round the corner of the barn, but they instinctively drew back when they saw the man get out of the car and come walking back down the road.

"Now what's he doing?"

The man turned up the track towards them.

"Get back inside. Quick!" They scrambled for the safety of the combine harvester.

Inside the shoe the doors were sealed and the power turned down to its lowest. The children sat in scared silence. They heard his footsteps when he entered the barn. They heard him snooping about. And because they didn't hear him creep away, they stayed in the shoe that night. Eventually, sleep overtook them – broken, fitful sleep. They didn't wake up until well into Saturday morning.

# Chapter Seventeen

**VILLAGE FETE**

Babysitting Fabian on Saturday morning had not been as dire as Stacey had expected it to be. Gaynor-down-the-road returned from the hairdresser with a scarf tied loosely round her new hairdo. She said she wasn't sure what her Derek would think of it, but it made her feel different.

"Now! Where's my bootiful baby boy? 'Ow's he been?"

"Oh, he was fine once he got used to you not being here! In fact he's been great!" Stacey, who had answered the door, took Gaynor into the garden.

Jon had put Fabian in a large cardboard box and was pushing him round the lawn, making noises like a steam engine. Fabian was shrieking with laughter and every time Jon stopped, he yelled "More!" It was a word Fabian knew well.

It had turned out to be a lovely sunny day and the garden was full of perfume. Gaynor smiled joyfully when she saw how happy her baby was. She had fully expected to find that he had been crying all morning. But here he was laughing, fit to bust! "Oh you are good children, looking after my little dumpling so well. I 'aven't seen 'im so jolly since... since..." She frowned, trying to remember, "since 'e was born really..."

She whipped off her scarf, to reveal a mop of orange spiky hair. Stacey and Jon stared. Fabian stared. His mouth turned down at the corners. He did not like this new version of his mum. It was frightening. He began to whimper. Jon ran and plucked a leaf from one of Stacey's bushes and tucked it into Fabian's fat little fist. It happened again. Just as it did the first time. The baby began to smile. He held his arms out to Gaynor, who took him with a cooing noise. "Well you kids 'ave been marvellous!" She found her purse and dug in. Handing Stacey a folded note, she said "'Ere Stacey luv, you deserve it." She dug back in her purse and turned to Jon. "So've you Jonathan. 'Ere's some for you too!"

They couldn't believe it. She'd given Stacey ten pounds – and Jon five!

"It's your leaves, Stacey! They're magic! I know they're magic!"

"They're not magic Jon! And they're still growing. You really shouldn't just pick them whenever you feel like it! Fabian would probably have been all right, even if you hadn't put that leaf in his hand."

"No he wouldn't. He was gonna cry and the leaf made him feel better again! They're magic, Stacey, honestly!"

Stacey didn't say anything. There was something rather special about those little shrubs – which were growing bigger almost as you looked at them.

Jon was carrying on. "You could find all the sick people in the village and make them better, I bet, with some of those leaves!"

"Oh calm down, Jon. They probably normally grow

in some rain forest. They say that lots of medicines come from plants that grow in the rain forests."

"No, they're magic!" insisted Jon.

*

Peter Farr took his children to the village fete that Saturday afternoon. It was a noisy, messy, colourful affair. Jon took his shoes off and had a great time jumping about on the bouncy castle. Dad bought them both candy floss. Stacey went to various stalls and for twenty pence a go, guessed the weight of the cake and the name of a huge teddy bear. Not that she wanted a stupid great teddy, but Jonathan might like it if she won. She would have paid to guess the number of twenty pence pieces in a jar, but at that point her friend, Gemma, came up with her younger sister, Hannah. The three drifted round together for a while until Gemma's dad came to take the two sisters for their riding lesson.

"See you Monday Stace!" Gemma turned and waved as she and Hannah followed their dad back to the family car.

Stacey wandered off, quite happy in her own company. She found a stall that was selling new but slightly damaged clothing. There was a lime green T-shirt which was her size, and as there seemed to be nothing much wrong with it, she bought it using some of the money Gaynor had given her. Next, she stopped at a refreshment stall which was being run by her PE teacher.

Miss Wilson was a popular teacher. She was always doing things for charity. Sponsored walks, sponsored runs, sponsored swims. Stacey and Gemma were convinced that all the male teachers were in love with her. Whenever they turned up to do their bit at these sports events, it seemed that nearly all the men from the school were there too, falling over themselves to help her. The girls would exchange loaded looks. Not surprising really, Miss Wilson was drop-dead gorgeous – and of course super fit.

"Hello Stacey, enjoying yourself?"

"Yes thanks Miss Wilson – d'you want any help?"

"You can pour orange squash into cups for me if you like." Stacey nipped behind the trestle table with its cans, cartons and cups of drinks. Feeling very useful and important, she began to measure out orange squash into plastic tumblers.

"Bought anything nice?" asked Miss Wilson, nodding at the paper bag which Stacey had stowed under the table.

"Just a top – I'll show it to you in a minute." They dealt with a few thirsty customers and then Stacey showed Miss Wilson her new purchase.

"Green's a good colour for you Stacey. Compliments your red hair."

When they'd had no customers for a while and Stacey felt she had out-served her usefulness, she picked up her bag and told Mrs Wilson that she was going to have another look round.

"That's fine Stacey, thanks for your help. Oh, before you go, would you mind putting this notice up on your gate? My little cat has gone missing and I'm trying to put notices up in various places, in case anyone has seen her." Stacey, studying the photocopy of a tabby kitten, said yes, she'd put the notice up. But it occurred to her that as she lived in the last house at the bottom of Mulberry Lane, hardly anyone would see it.

Miss Wilson had given her a carton of apple juice. She went and sat beneath a tree to drink it.

"Hot enough for you?" A young man was sitting not far away from her, eating an ice cream.

"Yeah..." Stacey didn't particularly feel like talking to a stranger.

"Hope you don't mind my asking, but doesn't your mum work at the lab at Ferndean?"

"Er... yes," she replied carefully. "You know her?"

"I was working with her last year. My name is Rob. You must be Stacey!"

Stacey was excited. So this was Rob! She studied him, trying to collect her thoughts. He had an open, pleasant face – with clear brown eyes and dark hair cropped close to his head. Finally, she answered, "Yeah... mum spoke about you – quite a lot. But I thought you went back to New Zealand?!"

"I did, but the crisis blew over and I was able to return to England. My job was still open."

"So you're still working at the lab?" asked Stacey.

"Yes I am."

Stacey stared at him. She wanted to say, "Then perhaps as someone who worked with her, you can tell me where she's gone?" but somehow she couldn't get it out. She felt a lump at the back of her throat. What did he know about her missing mum? She had only to ask him. But instead, she just sucked on her straw until a loud gurgle told her the carton was empty.

Rob crossed the small patch of grass between them and looked down at her with an anxious expression.

"She's not back yet, is she?" he asked quietly.

Stacey stared up at him, the sun making her eyes smart.

"Of course she's not back! Do you think I'd be sitting here on my own, if she was?"

"Maybe not," replied Rob. His voice was subdued.

"Of *course* I wouldn't be! My mum's been missing for a year – if she'd come back I wouldn't let her out of my sight!" She got to her feet, angrily crushing the empty carton in her hands and looking as though she might throw it at him.

Rob had taken a step back, as so many people did when confronted with a raging Stacey. "I'm sorry Stacey, I didn't mean to upset you – "

"Well you *do* upset me. You were working with her – you must know where she's gone!"

Rob didn't answer and his silence infuriated Stacey even more. "I *knew* it! You know where she is, don't you? *DON'T* you?!" She thrust her face into his, her eyes blazing.

Rob still didn't say anything but as Stacey stared into his eyes, the sounds around her became muted and the sun seemed to go behind a cloud. More than that, for the merest moment everything became dark – and instead of Rob's eyes, she beheld a planet like a great blue pearl, suspended in space.

Then everything was suddenly normal again. It was Stacey's turn to step back. *What was that? Did she imagine it?* She was confused and disarmed. Not daring to meet his eyes any longer, she looked down at her feet. "Anyway, how did you know who I was?" she asked sullenly.

"Your mum showed me some photos of you and your little brother. Your hair is longer, but it's still the same striking colour!"

"I hate it!" she replied, kicking a hole in the grass with her trainer. "And you know where my mum is, but you won't tell me, so I hate you too!"

"No you don't." He held out his hand for the squashed drink carton. "Here, give me that. I'll get you another."

Stacey carried on kicking a hole in the grass, bewildered and miserable, until a few seconds later Rob returned with a can of ice-cold cola. Without saying thank you, she pulled the ring and took a long swig. She found its cold sweetness soothing.

"Did you have a go at guessing the number of twenty pence pieces in that jar?" Rob asked casually.

Stacey shook her head.

"Go and have a guess. They'll be closing down in a minute!" He gave her a little push. "Go on!"

She started reluctantly toward the stall in question.

"Oh – and Stacey!" She turned, still glowering at him. "Catch!" A small silver coin came spinning through the air and landed in the grass at her feet. "It's twenty pence per guess!"

"Huh!" muttered Stacey, picking it up.

"Put down the first number that comes into your head!"

She was the last one to have a guess. She wrote down seventy-seven and put her name and address beside it.

# Chapter 18

## MULBERRY LANE

She dawdled off to find Jon. He was back on the bouncy castle with Ben, seeing who could jump the highest. His face was bright red and he was sweating. Stacey called, "You'd better get your shoes, I think it's probably time we went home!"

And as if to support this, her dad arrived behind her saying,"C'mon you two, let's go home. Good grief Jonathan, you're as red as a beetroot!"

"Dad can Ben come to tea?"

"Yep. But he must make sure it's OK with his mum and dad first!" Ben was putting on his shoes. He'd guessed the name of the teddy correctly – George – which was Ben's middle name. The teddy – almost as big as Ben – was invited to tea as well.

Just as they were leaving the fete, a cheery female voice came over the loud speaker system: "THIS IS TO ANNOUNCE THAT THE WINNER OF THE JAR OF TWENTY PENCE PIECES IS.... STACEY FARR! CORRECTLY GUESSING THE NUMBER OF TWENTY PENCE PIECES AT SEVENTY-SEVEN, STACEY GETS THE WHOLE JARFUL – FIFTEEN POUNDS AND FORTY PENCE WORTH – WELL DONE STACEY!"

Stacey, slightly light-headed, went and collected her prize to a smattering of applause, all the time scanning the crowd to see if she could see Rob. She had the absurd feeling that he had somehow caused her to win. But... even if he had known the amount of coins in the jar... he didn't put the number seventy-seven in her head! Did he?

Entering Mulberry Lane from the High Street, there were houses only on the left. On the right, there were shrubs and trees. The Farrs lived in the last house, at the bottom. Beyond that, the lane continued into open countryside past fields – the nearest one having horses in it. So it wasn't unusual to see a horsebox parked at the end of the lane. The children barely glanced at it.

*

Earlier that Saturday morning Brod, Mab, Treo and Jay woke up stiff and tired. They'd had a bad night, not just because of the snooper, but because Ean had been talking in her sleep. They had taken it in turns to soothe her, bathing her face with cool sponges and giving her drinks of water trying to make her comfortable. They could only hope that the snooper had gone – and didn't hear anything. It was decided that they should re-mask, leave the barn and find somewhere to park in the village. Preferably near to the Farrs' house.

Just as they were about to get MAD to change though, a group of kids from the village came into the barn. They weren't much interested in the combine-harvester, apart from noting that it hadn't been there before. They used the barn as a hiding place to smoke cigarettes, tell each other dirty jokes and generally think up tricks they could play on the other kids in the village. One of the boys was Darren Sprike's big brother and it wasn't long before he was encouraging his mates to do something nasty to Stacey and Jonathan Farr.

At the mention of the name 'Farr' those inside the shoe pricked up their ears. The chatter was not very distinct, so Treo activated the spy plate. This made it possible to see and hear clearly whatever was going on outside.

It became clear that they intended to collect up any dog dirt they could find, and smear it all over the Farr's gate and front door. They would do it after dark – and then when one of them came out on Sunday morning, they would get covered. They all thought it was a great joke. There was a lot of sniggering. Treo came away from the spy plate.

"Ugh, *gross*! We can't let them do that!"

The village gang left the barn and ambled off noisily down the track.

"OK that's settled it." declared Brod. "We park as close to the Farrs' house as possible..."

"...and catch them red handed!" said Treo.

"We'll think up something really revolting to do to them!" Jay was grinning wickedly.

"...and then we must go and find the seeds – or leaves!" finished Mab.

MAD had thought up another masterpiece. A horsebox in a Hampshire village is typical. By late afternoon it was parked at the end of Mulberry Lane opposite number eight. Inside, its young passengers spent their time caring for the invalid, eating the last of their food supplies and updating their journals – until night fell.

As dusk was falling, Mab slipped out of the shoe, crossed the road and walked through a gate into the field next to number eight. She sauntered along the hedgerow which was almost as tall as she was and looked over into the Farrs' garden.

She smelt them before she saw them. Their beautiful, familiar fragrance filled her every sense and brought her such a feeling of peace that she couldn't keep it to herself. She quickly returned to the shoe, opening the cab door on the side that was hidden from the house.

"C'mon everyone, you haven't been out all day. Come and breath the evening air – Ean will be all right for a few minutes."

"What if someone sees us?" Treo objected.

"They'll just think it's a bunch of kids playing in the field!" Mab replied. That did it. All four slipped out, crossed the road and entered the meadow.

"Walk close to the hedge," whispered Mab. And walking close to the hedge, they filled themselves with the glorious perfume of the healing leaves. Peeping over the hedge they saw, across the garden, eight thriving plants covered with tiny white flowers.

"Stacey must have planted them at least two days ago if they're in flower already," Brod said in a low voice. "We have to get into the garden as soon as possible – and get some leaves for Ean."

At that moment, the back door opened and two small boys came into the garden. One of them was chattering enthusiastically to the other. "...an' as soon as she watered them, they started to grow an' grow – an' now they've got flowers on them – an' Stacey only planted them a couple of days ago!" Jonathan ran over to Stacey's row of plants. "Smell them, smell them!" he cried, dancing around excitedly.

"I *can* smell them!" Ben said.

"No, no, put your face right near them – go on!" and Jonathan gave Ben a shove. Ben fell forward and landed with his face in one of the bushes.

The four, spying from behind the hedge, had ducked down a little so they couldn't be seen, but they found themselves slowly standing up again and watching. Ben got to his feet, then promptly sat down on the grass. He could hear things. Animals talking to one another, birds murmuring in their sleep. He even thought he could hear the grass growing. It felt strange and – beautiful. Then, beyond the gentle mumble of nature getting on with its business he could hear something more urgent. He had been going to thump Jonathan for pushing him but now – something was calling him.

"Listen!"

"What?"

"Can you hear that?" Ben started to look around him. The children bobbed down behind the hedge again.

"Hear what!" Jonathan replied impatiently. "I can't hear anything!"

"It's an animal, calling for help!"

"No it's not, Ben. It's Stacey singing."

"It's coming from the field! It's a small animal – and it's crying for help!"

At the mention of the word 'field', Mab, Brod, Treo and Jay, keeping low, scuttled back down the length of the hedge, across the road and vanished inside the horsebox.

# Chapter Nineteen

**MIRACLE**

Ben insisted on responding to the emergency that only he was aware of – and Jonathan went with him. It was growing darker. The horses in the field were just outlines, but the two boys were wholly absorbed in a rescue mission and didn't give it a thought. They had got about halfway across the field when Jonathan could hear it too and by this time the sound was recognisable. It was the mewing of a cat.

They found it under the bushes in the far corner. It was a tabby kitten and it had been injured. Ben took off his sweatshirt and using it as a blanket, gently scooped the kitten into his arms.

"D'you want me to carry it?" asked Jonathan.

"No, I'm fine," Ben said, cradling the little animal, which was now quiet. "D'you think it's dead?"

"I don't think so, but it looks badly hurt."

Then they heard the voice of Jonathan's dad calling them. Jonathan started to run, knowing he was in trouble. Ben continued to walk carefully with his fragile burden. Dad was cross.

"Where the *hell* have you been Jon?"

"We heard this..."

"Get inside! Where's Ben?"

"He's coming dad. Dad, we heard this..."

"I'M RESPONSIBLE FOR BEN WHILE HE'S IN MY CARE. WHAT MADE YOU THINK YOU COULD JUST RUN OFF INTO THE FIELDS WITHOUT TELLING ME?"

"We heard this...."

"WHERE THE **HELL** IS BEN?"

"*DAD, I'M TRYING TO TELL YOU!! BEN HEARD THIS ANIMAL OUT IN THE FIELD CRYING FOR HELP AND WE HAD TO GO AND RESCUE IT!!*" And then he added in a normal voice, "It's a kitten dad, and it's hurt!"

Ben arrived in the garden with the kitten at about the same time as Stacey came out to see what was happening. They all crowded round to see.

"Poor little thing." Dad gently touched its fur. "It must have been run over – or maybe a fox got it..."

"I wonder if it's Miss Wilson's kitten that's been missing?" Stacey suddenly said. "I'll go and get the picture she gave me this afternoon."

It was indeed Miss Wilson's kitten. Dad phoned one of the school governors to see if he could get her telephone number. The three children peered at the kitten which looked lifeless, and suddenly Ben started to cry.

"I think it's dead... it's gone all floppy..." Jonathan bit his lip and looked at Stacey.

"Shall we try some of your leaves, Stacey?"

Stacey shrugged. "I don't think it will make much difference Jon, but maybe it's better than doing nothing."

Once back in the garden, they laid the kitten on the grass as near to the bushes as they could. Then picking lots of leaves and a few of the flowers they sprinkled them over the small, furry body. They held their breath and waited. Nothing happened. They sat on the grass, watching intently. The body remained lifeless. Ben began to sob. Jonathan hung his head, and Stacey knew he was crying too.

"I'm sorry." She felt almost responsible that the leaves hadn't worked. "I'm really sorry, but I did say that it wouldn't make much difference didn't I?"

"Oh shut up, Stace – you always know everything, don't you?"

Wisely, Stacey kept quiet.

They heard the telephone ringing in the house and dad answering it. A moment or two later he came into the garden. "Miss Wilson's out but I've left a message on her Ansaphone. Ben, your mum's just rung. I didn't realize how late it was. I told her I'd take you straight home. Come on sunshine." He went back inside and Ben slowly got to his feet, sniffing. Stacey was dreading having to break the news to Miss Wilson that her kitten was dead.

"Shall we take it inside?" asked Jonathan. They all turned and looked. It seemed appropriate to leave the body there, in the fragrant garden, strewn with leaves and flowers.

"Let's leave it there, shall we? At least for now," Stacey said. And the three of them trooped sadly back down the garden path.

It was very annoying of Ben, who was in front, to stop so suddenly on the back door step. The other two nearly tripped over him. There were cross exclamations, but Ben said, "Sssshh!!"

Obediently they shushed. There was dead silence.

"What?" said Jonathan.

"Listen!" answered Ben.

"I am listening – and there's nothing!"

"No you're not! Be quiet!"

Stacey suddenly felt spooked and a shiver went down her spine. Then she heard it. The faintest "Mew!"

"It's the kitten!" Ben whispered.

"Ben, the kitten is dead! It's probably another cat you can hear!"

"It's the kitten!" Ben repeated. His face was as white as a sheet. Stacey saw that he had goose pimples. Then they saw it.

Walking up the path and into the light that came from the kitchen window, came a small, tabby kitten. It still had leaves in its fur and there was a white petal on the end of its nose. With great dignity it walked past them and into the kitchen, where it jumped up onto dad's favourite chair and sat licking itself clean.

# Chapter Twenty

## SPRIKE'S GANG

Inside the shoe the four children were getting seriously bored. They had been keeping themselves occupied with playing word games, mind games and card games and their journals were up to date. There was nothing to do but wait. But they were heartily sick of it. There was no more food and they were hungry. To get Ean well again and back on her feet was becoming ever more urgent.

"Not that we want Ean to get better just because we're hungry," said Jay, as they discussed the situation together, "but she will know how to go about getting more food."

"And she will get us back on track with our assignment!" added Brod.

It was Treo's turn to keep watch through the spy plate. They were waiting for developments. Some of the village gang were plotting a nasty trick to play on the Farrs – which they were going to stop. Most importantly they were waiting for the Farr family to go to bed, so that they could sneak into their back garden and get some healing leaves for Ean. Once Ean was better, she would know what their next move should be.

Mab was sitting with Ean and looked up as Treo said,

"Something's happening at number eight!" All eyes went to the spy plate. Treo switched up the volume and adjusted the night viewer.

They stopped whatever they were doing to listen and watch. The Farrs and Ben were spilling out of the front door.

"...Really great to hear that it's alive and well, but it simply is not possible for a handful of leaves from a bush – however exotic – to cause a cat to be resurrected!" Dad was speaking in that nasty, squashing way which adults have, when they want foolish young people to be reasonable.

"It was dead, dad. We saw it!"

"I was holding it in my arms," said Ben, "and I felt it die."

Dad just shook his head and smiled wisely. Again, Stacey kept quiet but her thoughts were rioting.

"I said Stacey's bushes were magic!" Jonathan was punching the air.

"Pipe down Jon, and get in the car. Stace, you'd better get in the front. The back seat is full up with two boys and a teddy bear." Dad lowered his window and backed out of the driveway.

The last thing children in the shoe heard as it drove past the horsebox was, "No Ben, I don't think teddy bears need safety belts, but you can fasten him in if you want to."

"They've discovered the power of the leaves," said Jay.

"The parent doesn't believe the children's story... but if we leave them where they are, it won't be long before he discovers for himself." Treo began to bite her nails.

"Well, they're all out. Now would be a good time to go in and get some leaves," said Mab.

It was at that point though, that the Sprike gang – seeing all the lights off at number eight, and no car outside – decided to strike. There were five of them – including Darren Sprike and his big brother. He had a plastic carrier bag and a small spade. The children in the shoe wouldn't have heard them, but those in the gang weren't being particularly quiet. There was a lot of sniggering.

Jay stood at the spy plate, and reported to the others, who were poised over the console with horrible smiles on their faces. As the older Sprike brother – who they called Wayne – put his hand on the Farr's iron gate, an electric charge passed through it. Wayne shot backwards through the air and managed to bring at least two of the others down with him.

Darren Sprike decided he would have a go. He tried to climb over the fence. Treo waited until he was sat nicely astride, before she released a similar current of electricity. Darren fell off the fence, clutching himself and howling. Further down the road curtains twitched. Darren's howl had brought one or two of the neighbours to their windows. By now, Jay was laughing so loudly, that the others told him to shut up or he'd give the game away!

After ten minutes or so, not wanting to give up, another member of the gang, a girl they called Cat, sneaked into number seven's garden and vaulted over their hedge into number eight. But setting foot on the Farr's path was another mistake. It was as slippery as ice – she couldn't stay on her feet – twice she slipped over. She moved off the path and, walking over the flower bed, tried to reach the front door.

It was Mab who brought the lion to life. There was a cast iron lion's head on the door, the door knocker being between its teeth. As Cat approached, the lion's head began to glow. Softly growling, it turned and stared, with eyes of fiery red. The growling got louder – and Cat fled, dropping the spade and the carrier bag. She hared across the grass and leapt over the fence. The boys stood in the roadway looking back at number eight, exclaiming with disbelief.

"Language please!" smirked Treo.

"Shall we finish them off?" Jay asked, and without waiting for an answer, he reached over and jabbed at the defence panel.

Of course it was the last straw for the Sprike gang. They felt a strange, cold tingling, and then to their utter amazement, as they stood there, their clothes began to dissolve. In trying to stop it happening, they clutched at their jeans, their shirts. But they just melted away under their hands. They had begun to run. But by the time they reached the village end of Mulberry Lane, they had very little more than their underwear on.

Back inside the shoe the children were still laughing. They had been so fed up with waiting around, being anxious about Ean's sickness, anxious about remaining out of sight, anxious about running out of food. Putting one over on Sprike's gang had been wonderful – like a release for their pent up feelings.

But as the laughter died down and they shut off the defence system, the children had the uneasy feeling that they might just have overdone it.

# Chapter Twenty One

## THE HEALING OF EAN

Still, it made a great topic of conversation, and the children re-lived the past half hour over and over again. At one point Treo observed that perhaps they had been unfair, using Home Planet technology to defeat a handful of clueless Earth children.

"But they were *nasty,* clueless Earth children. They had it coming to them!" said Mab.

The Farrs came home, and in the shoe they heard Mr Farr telling his children that they should go straight to bed as soon as they got in. There was a lot of grumbling and they heard Stacey say, "It's not fair dad! I wanted to be up when Miss Wilson comes for the kitten!"

"She may not even be coming tonight Stace..." and then the front door closed.

Two hours passed before Stacey's dad went to bed and they hoped that when all the lights were off, it meant he was asleep. Mab decided she must be the one to creep into their garden and get the leaves. She was nervous about being caught, even though she knew that it was most unlikely.

As she was thinking though, Brod spoke up. "I've been wondering about how to get nearer to the plants.

We could drive through the gate into the field and park right next to the hedge, overlooking their back garden."

"You don't think the noise would wake Mr Farr up?" Mab asked.

"We can silence the motor though, can't we?" Then he slipped into her mind. *"From the time you leave the shoe, we will communicate in thought only."*

Mab smiled at him cheekily and sent back: *"I had already decided to do that!"*

Treo was staring at Mab and Brod, her eyes narrowed. "You two are mind talking, aren't you?"

The two, slightly embarrassed, admitted it.

Treo and Jay looked at each other and started to laugh. "Treo and I have been on thinking-terms since yesterday! When we were parked behind the barn and discovered we were being spied on, Treo jumped into my mind with a shriek!"

"The truth is... " Treo interrupted, jabbing Jay in the ribs with her elbow, "I saw the snooper first, and setting up a mental link with Jay was the most subtle way of letting him know!"

"That means none of us has to worry about popping into each other's minds, if there is a need!" said Mab.

"And while Mab is collecting leaves, it goes without saying, that if a warning becomes necessary, it should be done..."

Brod paused as the others chimed in with, "..mentally!"

The next thing was to move the shoe. It was driven silently, through the gate of the field, and parked. A horsebox in a field of horses – parked so that all there was between them and Stacey's plants, was the hedge.

*

Mab half climbed, half fell over the hedge into the Farr's back garden. She got to her feet and stood listening. There was the soft hoot of an owl. Apart from that, utter silence. It was another moonlit night and Mab had no problem locating the plants. The fragrance of the healing leaves wafted over her.

Thoughts of home filled her mind. She saw the lovely green landscapes, the house where she lived, her family. She remembered her school – and the unique training she had undergone. She also recalled her assignment. Would her group be able to complete its mission? Between them they had done some pretty outrageous things, considering they were not meant to be traced. What about the way they had dealt with Sprike's gang? Would anyone believe their story? What about the kitten that came back to life? Unlikely happenings, unbelievable happenings – but all stemming from a particular location in a particular village. Very dangerous. She knew she would have to tell Ean the truth – and dreaded it.

Ean! Mab came to her senses. There was going to have to be some guess work here. Certainly the leaves would cure Ean. But how many leaves would they need? Just a handful? Lots? A whole plant? Mab picked a large bunch of sprigs, including some of the flowers, and stuffed them down the front of her shirt where they tickled horribly. She clambered back over the hedge, trying to inflict as little damage as possible. The children were watching for her and opened up as soon as she got to the door.

They got busy stripping the leaves off their stalks and picking the flowers. Jay suddenly said, "OK – leave this to me please guys!"

The other three did as he asked, respectful of Jay's speciality. They were silent but their thoughts mingled, and they agreed with one another – it was ironic that the first person on Earth to benefit from Jay's skills was a Home-daughter! But what a good thing it was that they had someone on their team who was a healer.

Jay laid back the cover on Ean's bed.

"Mind if we watch?" asked Treo.

"Not at all, but please be very quiet."

"OK," whispered Brod.

Jay put Ean's arms at her side and turned them, so that her hands were palm up. He pulled the pillow under Ean's head further down – so that it was under her neck – and her chin pointed upwards. "Treo, turn on one of the heat panels and warm a cloth for me will you?"

No-one noticed the shoe expand, as its artificial intelligence recognised a need for more space. Outside, against the night sky, it was just an ordinary horsebox.

Jay placed a leaf under each of Ean's armpits. Then one each on the inside creases of her elbows, one each on the insides of the wrists. He placed a few flowers in the hollow at the base of Ean's throat – and then asking Treo for the warm cloth, he placed leaves on either side of her neck and wrapped the warm fabric round them to keep them in place. Covering Ean over once more, Jay then placed three leaves across Ean's forehead. "Turn the heat panel off now Treo, we don't need it. Bring me a cold cloth, will you? And then turn the light down please." The light was turned down and Jay applied the cold cloth to Ean's forehead, covering the leaves. "You may as well go to bed you lot. It only takes one to keep watch, and I'd rather it was me."

"OK then, goodnight!" said Treo, quite happy to turn in.

"Wake me if you need help," Mab said – and followed Treo's example.

"G'night!" called Brod softly.

All of them were affected by the perfume of the leaves and they slept deeply. So it seemed as though the voice came from far off.

"Mab! Mab! Wake up!" Jay was shaking her shoulder.

"I'm asleep!" Mab groaned, shrinking beneath the cover.

"Not any more, you're not!" hissed Jay. "I'm sorry, Mab, but you did say to wake you if I needed help. I just can't keep my eyes open any longer. Now get up, or I'll tickle you!"

Mab got up. "How's Ean?"

"She's doing fine. Pulse and temperature are stable. And she's sleeping normally. I just feel it would be good if someone sat with her, in case she wakes up. D'you mind?"

Shaking her head and yawning, Mab shuffled across and took over from Jay, who was soon in bed and fast asleep.

Before she sat with Ean, Mab gazed through the spy plate for a while. It was just beginning to get light outside. She wondered if she would be able to stay awake and looked around for something to occupy her mind.

A voice said, "When did we last talk to watch captain?"

Mab turned to see Ean, propped up on one elbow, looking as though she had just woken up from a good night's sleep.

# Chapter Twenty Two

**IDENTITIES**

"Ean!"

Ean found herself being hugged with great enthusiasm. "You're better! The leaves did their work!"

"How long have I been ill?"

"It seems like forever, but actually it's just two days. We discovered you were poorly on Friday morning and contacted watch captain. She said you were probably suffering from journey fatigue, and that we should find somewhere quiet and hang around for a day or so to give you chance to recover. We have been pretty scared, I can tell you!"

"So we're still somewhere quiet, are we?"

"No-o-o!" Mab said slowly. "We came to a place where we could find something to make you better."

Ean's eyes narrowed. "Now why does that make me feel uneasy? You said just now the leaves did their work – was that the 'something' to make me better?"

"Er, yes."

"What leaves would those be, Mab?" And as Ean said this, a leaf – which had been stuck to her forehead – fluttered onto her cover. Mab was silent as Ean picked it up and recognised it with a little exclamation. "Where on Planet Earth do healing leaves grow? I think you'd better tell me where we are, Mab – and how we are masked!"

"We are a method of transport for carrying horses, and we are parked in a field – a different field from the one you parked in two days ago of course!"

"So, we're a horsebox in a field. You'd better tell me where the field is and how we got here. But first Mab, make us both a nice drink will you?"

Mab made them both a drink, whilst Ean picked leaves off her arms and brushed them onto to the floor. As she poured hot water onto fruit tea, she mentioned that they had run out of food.

"That can soon be sorted. Now come and sit down, Mab. There is enough of the night left.... start talking!"

So Mab talked. She left nothing out. Starting her account with how she had brought seeds to Earth, she told Ean about her decision to get rid of them. How she had tossed them into Mr Bascombe's van. She spoke about their anxiety over Ean's illness, and how first she had told Brod of what she had done, then Treo and Jay. She described their trip to Hollybrook, to find Mr Bascombe's van, in the hope that it might still have the seeds in it.

Ean listened very carefully, with a grave expression on her face. But somewhere deep in Ean's eyes, Mab thought she detected a twinkle. Of course she must be imagining it. How would Ean find anything to laugh at in their performance of the last two days? But when Mab came to the bit in Mr Bascombe's shop and did her imitation of Mr Bascombe, the twinkle became pronounced and Ean had to cover her mouth to stop herself laughing out loud.

When it came to how Stacey Farr had bought the seeds and taken them home and planted them, Ean covered her face with both hands. At first Mab thought she was laughing again, but suddenly there was a sob. "I'm so sorry Ean, I didn't think for a minute that anyone would actually get hold of them and plant them! What can I say, except I'm sorry – I'm so sorry..." Then suddenly she understood why Ean was so upset – and she was filled with shame.

"Ean! Will we have to abort the mission?" And Mab, biting her lip, began to cry. It was all her fault. She had brought seeds to Earth – and now all the globeringers would have to be recalled.

"I don't know if we will have to abort the mission, Mab. You were wrong not to check your pockets. It's just that kind of mistake that we were afraid of. That's why we made the rule. But strangely, things may yet work out well. Now stop crying. Come on."

"But you were crying!" exclaimed Mab.

"Was I?" Ean wiped a tear from her cheek. "So I was! Well it was for another reason entirely, so do cheer up! You have to tell me the rest – and it's nearly daytime!"

So Mab plodded on with her story. Ean looked very disturbed about the snooper. And when the resurrected kitten came into the story, followed by their treatment of the Sprike gang, she was aghast. "I'm beginning to doubt if we will remain undetected!"

Mab looked at her hands and felt wretched – again.

"So tell me Mab, we are parked right outside the garden of this Farr family?" As she spoke, Ean's voice trembled.

Mab glanced up at Ean's face. "Yes," she whispered.

117

"You see..." Ean seemed to be speaking with difficulty and Mab wondered if she was ill again. "You see... it's not just globeringer shoes that can mask." Mab looked confused.

Just then a sound made her look through the spy plate. She saw the Farr's back door open. Stacey came out cradling a tabby kitten in her arms. It was a beautiful Sunday morning. Without turning round Mab asked, "You said 'It's not just globeringer shoes that can mask' – why did you say that?"

"Because people can be masked Mab. I am masked."

Mab gave a puzzled laugh. "*You* are masked – how?"

"I am not really from Home Planet. I am from Earth."

Mab swung round to face Ean. "But that's not true! You came from Home with us. You were on our training course!"

"Oh yes, I came here from Home Planet, but I don't belong there. I belong here. I am an Earth scientist. I've been part of an experiment set up between certain agencies on Home Planet and Earth."

Mab stared at Ean, open-mouthed.

"And that's not all." Ean peered through the spy plate and her gaze rested on Stacey and the kitten "That little girl out there... is my daughter."

# Chapter Twenty Three

## BROD'S RUN

Brod had heard everything. At first he just lay there listening, as Mab related the bizarre events of the last two days. He found himself wanting to laugh at the same time as Ean did, and was tempted to sit up and join in. Instead he kept his eyes shut, characteristically keeping out of it, and tried to guess what Mab was going to say next. When Ean revealed who she really was though, he was stunned. They had been entrusted to the care of an Earth person! He didn't know quite how he felt about that. Home Planet people and Home Planet technology – in the hands of a human. He would never have guessed it, to look at Ean, but her Earth identity would explain why she had been ill.

She could only have travelled to Home Planet in a far-reacher. And she could only have got to the far-reacher in a globeringer shoe. So she must have made the trip when the last mental energists had come home from Earth. The experiment she spoke of must obviously be authorised – but why? What happened to the rules? Rules made to prevent them from being traced? There must now be people on Earth who knew about the existence of Home Planet. The whole idea of keeping their existence secret was to prevent Earth from trying to reach Home, thus contaminating it. Earth people were destructive. It must be like... Brod tried to simplify it in his mind. It must be like... kissing someone who was sick. The contact could do nothing but harm.

After waiting a little, he pretended to have just woken up. Mab seemed unaffected by the revelation of Ean's identity. But then she had brought seeds to Earth, and upset the whole mission. So she was probably relieved to find out that her group leader was as devious as she was.

Brod didn't think about how stressed they all were. He didn't remember that they were very hungry – and that these factors alone would make him angry – when normally he might have reacted more logically. He got up and prepared to go out.

"Where are you going, Brod?" Ean asked.

"Out," was the short reply.

Ean tried to coax a greeting out of him, cheerfully suggesting, "Well *hello* Ean! How are you today? Glad to see you looking so much better!"

He didn't respond, just stuffed his feet into his shoes and reached for the opening mechanism on the door.

Ean narrowed her eyes at him. "Where do you think you're going?"

"I must have fresh air!"

"All in good time. First, we need to discuss what we're going to do!" Ean put a hand on his arm. "Let's have a drink, and then we'll go and get some breakfast!"

Brod shook her hand off. "It's all right, Ean, I don't want to keep you from your family!"

Ean nodded slowly, knowing he'd overheard her conversation with Mab.

"Brod, there is an important contact I have to make before I can see my family. We also have to get more food. Now is not the time to leave the shoe, especially on your own! Brod!"

He had pulled away from her, and was out of the door.

"Shall I go after him?" asked Mab.

"No. I can't afford to have an incident so near to my home! He'll soon come to his senses. He's stressed out and hungry – aren't we all?"

Mab stared at the closed door, dismayed. "Will he be safe out there?"

"Not particularly..."

*

Brod walked down Mulberry Lane and into the village. He felt very, very strange. Breathing deeply, his long legs striding out, he took the road past the shops, to the end of the High Street, where there was a tall grey building with a spire. A loud jangling noise came from its roof, as people filed down the path and were swallowed up in its gloomy interior.

"Church!" Brod muttered, identifying what he had only ever seen in pictures before now. He stood by the gate and watched, fascinated. A large red-faced man came along with a woman holding his arm. It was Mr Bas-combe. Not wanting to be recognised, Brod dived across the road without looking. A bike almost ran into him and he was given a shrill ticking off by an old woman. She had a small dog in a basket on the front of the bike, and it barked furiously. Brod backed off, apologising.

He was well past the church when the realisation came to him that he was being followed. He had been conscious of it since he had turned out of Mulberry Lane, but he had been so preoccupied, that only now did it become obvious. He continued to walk, aware of someone's presence a few yards behind him. And the mind of that someone was intent on catching up with him.

"Stay calm, stay calm!" he told himself, as he quickened his pace. But he was scared. He had just found out that there were people on Earth who knew of the existence of Home. Was it possible that the secret had leaked out? Of course it might just be some ordinary human, wanting to talk to him, be friends with him. But he could feel that mind, nudging at the edge of his own – and he knew it wasn't an ordinary human.

It could be Intercept. But Intercept was a human organisation, and whoever was behind him did not seem human. He glanced round. The last stragglers were turning down the pathway to the church. On a low wall, next to the gate, sat an old man. He appeared harmless, just an old human, sitting enjoying the sunshine. But Brod felt sure that the old man was the one whose mind was stalking him. He was just about to turn back to see where he was going when the old man lifted his head and caught Brod's gaze.

The eyes were not old. They were young eyes – dark, burning eyes – in an ageing face. A sudden terror gripped Brod. He started to run away down the road and out towards the open country.

*"That's right Brod, you run..."* a cold voice slithered into his mind. *"Go as far as you can. In fact you'll find*

122

*you can't stop. You've got good long legs. You should be able to make it as far as the quarry."*

Brod's legs were going like pistons – and it wasn't just fear that was driving him. He was being forced to run. He could hear his own heart beating, and the soft pounding of his feet on the road.

*"You're doing very well!"* the voice said behind him. *"The gate, the gate over the road, turn in..."* As he crossed the road, he tried to look back to see if the old man was actually behind him, or whether it was just the mind that was following him. His head wouldn't turn. The only part of his body that would move was his legs.

They were taking him across a field, across two fields. His breath was beginning to come in gasps. He was trying to think. His pursuer must be a mental energist. He could project his thoughts – and disturbingly – those thoughts were in the Home tongue.

Brod was a Mental-Energist too. But he was allowing blind terror take hold of him and he could no longer control his thoughts. Coming to terms with this, he started to quell his fear. *"Get a grip, get a **grip**!"* he bullied himself. He summoned all his mental power and forced his legs to slow down. A dirt track led to the edge of an old quarry and there was a steep cliff-like drop over its side. He couldn't see the bottom but he knew it was a long way down.

*"Keep going!"* came the voice, and Brod's legs sped up again, scuffing up brown dust from the track. He was using all the power of his mind as a brake. Concentrating every thought on his moving body. *"Must stop! Must stop!"*

As he reached the edge of the quarry, he was able to

stop, but it was much too near for comfort. At that moment, his concentration was broken by the sound of a motorbike roaring up the track.

*"Jump!"* the voice commanded.

Brod threw himself over the edge.

# Chapter Twenty Four

## RESCUE

He screamed with his mind and his voice, as his balance went and his body began to plunge. Or it would have done, but at that split second, a strong hand grabbed his sleeve and, painfully, a chunk of his arm – hauling him back onto the path. He and his rescuer toppled over backwards onto the dirt. Brod lay there stunned, gasping. Somewhere, high in the sky above him, a lark twittered excitedly.

"You are one lucky son of a gun," said a normal, friendly voice beside him.

Brod flipped his head to one side. It was the motorcyclist. He was still laid flat on his back. "I thought I was dead," Brod replied, fighting the urge to cry. His heart was pounding. He was shaking uncontrollably.

"You looked as though you wanted to die, flinging yourself over the edge like that!"

"No... no... don't want to die!" He made himself sit up and take a few deep breaths.

"So what happened then? It certainly looked as if you had a death wish!"

"I must have slipped!" answered Brod lamely.

The motorcyclist sat up and stared at Brod's pale, dirty face. "Whatever!" he said. "D'you need a lift home?"

Brod surveyed the motorbike. He thought he might well enjoy a ride. But...

"No thanks."

"I don't think you should be left on your own. At least, not yet."

Brod thought how true that was, but he couldn't get the man to take him back to the horsebox.

"Tell you what, I'll give you a lift and drop you off at a point near your home. How about that?" And at Brod's nod of consent, he held out a hand and pulled him to his feet. "I also think we need to have a little talk."

Brod climbed onto the back of the motorbike behind his new friend and they crossed back over the two fields, onto the main road again. Before they reached the village, the bike turned off up a track and Brod recognised the old barn where they had previously parked the shoe. They came to a stop behind the barn and both dismounted. Brod was then invited to take a seat on an old oil drum, while his companion opened one of the cases on the side of his bike. He brought out a large flask and parcels of food from one of the panniers on the sides of his bike.

"Thirsty? This is apple juice."

Brod took the cup offered to him and drank. The juice was cloudy, cold and sweet. He was too thirsty to even think about comparing it with Home apple juice.

"There is food too. But first, tell me your story."

"I haven't got a story!" Brod screwed up his face as if begging the man not to ask.

"Of course you haven't. How could you possibly tell me the truth?" He opened the box and brought out fresh crusty bread and butter and some cheese. He offered it to Brod who took it after a small hesitation. "That's home made wholemeal bread, and the cheese is vegetarian. Go on, try it!" And as Brod still looked uncertain he continued, "Go on! And *I'll* tell you your story while you eat.

"I'll make this as simple and direct as I can. Two days ago you were parked on this very spot in a multi-passenger vehicle with shaded windows. You came to the village in search of something or someone – and parked where you thought you might not easily be seen, whilst you made plans on how to find what you were looking for.

"Two of your group were frightened by someone who they felt was spying on them from a car parked by the roadside. They moved the vehicle inside the barn. Later that night the spy came back, even entering the barn to see what he could find. That spy was me."

At this point, he broke into the Home tongue, but it didn't sound sinister, as it had when the old man had spoken. "I know your name is Brod. You arrived on Earth four days ago with the rest of your group. I have been keeping an eye out for you. But something went wrong with your mission and you didn't turn up quite when I expected. Like you, Brod, I am a mental energist. Instead of returning home a year ago I changed places – as part of a government sanctioned experiment – with the person with whom I made a mind-lock. She is also a scientist. She is your group leader – you know her as Ean, which is short for Elizabeth Ann. And before you dismiss her as a mere Earth person, Brod, I would inform you here and now that she is a woman of enormous courage – to the extent that she has been made an Honorary Home-daughter!"

Brod looked embarrassed but Rob grinned. "Before we do anything else, she has to make a report to her laboratory at Ferndean. Having done that, she will hand you kids over to me! My name is Rob. I am your new group leader."

*

Brod stared at Rob with astonishment. But his story tied in with Ean's – and it began to make sense. Now though, he was full of questions. "Why didn't you come and tell us who you were, instead of snooping around like you did?"

"I was instructed to make contact only with Ean when you arrived here. I knew that both the people carrier and the combine harvester were the shoe in different disguises." He showed Brod a small hand-held device. "An Electronic pulse."

Brod remembered. "Yeah – we learnt about those during training. There's one in the shoe. They can home in on all forms of Home Planet technology, no matter where they are – or how well masked."

"They also act as portable communicators."

"So you know where the shoe is now?"

"I have had a trace on it ever since it arrived in Hollybrook." Rob jerked his head at the bread in Brod's hand. "Eat that. It's good stuff. I made it myself."

Brod sank his teeth into the bread. It was very tasty.

Rob continued: "This morning I felt I really must make contact, so using the motorbike, I visited the horsebox and knocked on the door."

"I bet that scared them."

"The kids were a bit worried, but Ean very calmly called out, 'Who is it?' – and when I identified myself, she opened the door and dragged me inside!"

"Did she tell you I had gone off on my own?"

"She did. She and I have a lot to talk about. We also have to visit the laboratory at Ferndean. But you – *trouble!* – were priority. 'Go and find Brod!' she told me."

There was silence for a while. Brod felt ashamed.

Rob said, "I was seriously alarmed that you were out on your own. I unshuttered my mind and listened for your whereabouts. I just caught the undercurrent of your thoughts as you passed the church. Then I heard the other guy..."

"Yeah! Who was that walking nightmare, the old man who tried to kill me? He's a mental energist isn't he? And where did he go after you came on the scene?"

"He's some kind of Energist – has to be. I don't know who he is Brod. All I know is that he poses a threat to our existence – as if we didn't have enough to watch out for. As for where he is... I don't know that either!"

"Could you trace him with the pulse?"

"Only if he's using some kind of Home Planet device. I could do a mind search... but I'm worried that he may detect me."

"Where was he at the time you rescued me?"

"He was nearby. I didn't see him, though. He was so busy trying to make you commit suicide, I'm pretty certain he wasn't onto me. And your scream was so mind-blowing that its soundwaves would likely have masked my intervention. He may not know you are still alive and if I'm careful, he may not find out who I am either."

"He would have heard the bike though, wouldn't he?"

"Possibly. But I bet he doesn't know it was ridden by another mental energist!" Rob had been leaning against the motorbike. He stood up quickly. "We've got to get back to the shoe! Are you all right now, Brod?"

Brod gave a thumbs up and climbed onto the bike behind Rob.

# Chapter Twenty Five

## NEW ZEALANDERS

As Rob and Brod approached Mulberry Lane, a horsebox moved out of it and drove up the High Street ahead of them. The motorbike engine was so noisy that rather than shout, Brod, by-passing politeness, popped into Rob's mind: *"That's the shoe!"*

*"Yeah, I wonder what's caused them to move so suddenly?"*

*"You drive, Rob – I'll ask Mab. Excuse me..."* and extending his mind further, he jumped into Mab's.

*"Where are you going Mab?"*

*"Huh! You're a fine one to ask that question! Just follow, we're going somewhere to re-mask!"*

*"Why?"*

*"Ask one of the others, I'm trying to drive this thing!"*

*"Why? Where's Ean?"*

Treo broke in. *"Ean is a passenger, Brod. She didn't want to be seen by any of her family as we drove out of the field!"*

At that point, Rob, having himself caught the general drift of the mental interchange, pulled out and overtook the horsebox, signalling that *they* should follow *him*.

Twenty minutes later, inside a small wood, two adults and four children sat on the grass sharing Rob's food. Behind them stood the shoe, re-masked as a large camper. Rob's bike was parked next to it. There was a solemn atmosphere, as between them Brod and Rob recounted the morning's misadventure. Only Jay continued to chew, as Treo asked, "Who is this freaky old man?"

"We don't know, do we?" answered Brod, turning to Rob.

"I've had time to think about that... and I think there's only one possible explanation."

"What?" They all asked together.

"He's from Four Eighty-One."

Jay swallowed his last mouthful. "The Penal Planet? But how d'you know?"

"I don't. But he was willing to kill Brod in cold blood. He's a criminal."

Mab looked worried. "But how did he get to Earth from Four Eighty-One?"

"I dunno. He must have hi-jacked a ship."

Treo looked doubtful. "What, all by himself?"

There was a loaded silence. The thought that there may be more than one Home Planet criminal on the loose was not comforting. Then Ean spoke: "The bottom line is, guys, we have to be extremely careful. Eyes in the backs of our heads. Stay together." She gave Brod a meaningful look. "We have things to do. First, we must report to the lab at Ferndean that Rob and I have met up."

"We also have to tell Rob about the seeds... and your illness... and stuff." Mab added quietly.

"We do indeed," replied Ean, with a dry smile.

It became Rob's turn to listen, as Mab told him the story of the seeds, what had made her dispose of them and how they had ended up in Mr Bascombe's van. She spoke of Ean's illness and the group's decision – on learning about the seeds – to trace them. There was a grin on Brod's face as she described Mr Bascombe and how they found out where the seeds had gone. The fact that they had been planted and were growing healthily in Stacey's back garden caused Rob to gape. "That is some coincidence! That you should drop the seeds in a van which was destined for this village – and then that they should end up in... well... in Ean's back garden!"

"Hmm..." Ean was thoughtful. "It's almost as if they just didn't want to be disposed of."

"As if they had a mind of their own," Rob added, with a glint of humour.

Ean suddenly became business-like: "Well, we can't laze around here all day! We have to report to the lab. And then, I would very much like to see my family!"

Before they left, Rob wheeled his bike deep into the bushes and locked it, removing the carriers containing the food and stowing them inside the shoe. The children then put on earphones for speed-learning – and plugged into the console. Flicking past 'language' and 'English' they clicked on 'accents – New Zealand' then SPILL – and within seconds they spoke English with a New Zealand accent.

"You sound just like Rob now," Ean laughed. "Foreigners!"

"You'd better believe it!" said Rob.

## Chapter Twenty Six

### FOUR EIGHTY-ONE

Because of its position in the night skies above Home, the Penal Planet is simply known as Four Eighty-One. There are no prisons on Home Planet. When caught, thieves and fraudsters have to work for their victims, until they have replaced everything they have stolen, and generally made amends for of their crime. The harder they work, the sooner their punishment is done. The judicial system is quite involved, but it serves to keep the planet peaceful – and safe.

It is only the life-takers who end up on Four Eighty-One. There they work hard in the mines and industries which have grown up from the planet's mineral resources. It is a small, cold planet. Any parties working in the open air have to wear special cold weather suits. But the prisoners are well provided for. They are clothed and fed. There is opportunity for them to have recreation and exercise. There are libraries and classes in which any number of subjects can be learnt. Convicts can actually lead a reasonably pleasant life there, improving both body and mind. There is only one thing they can't have. Freedom. They are allowed visitors twice in a year, but there is no parole. And no returning Home.

Most prisoners resign themselves to spending their lives on Four Eighty-One. Apart from the fact that life is not bad, there is massive security. Any man or woman who wants to steal a ship and 'make a break for it' faces huge problems. There is only one major outport which is permanently electronically shielded. Guards are armed. Would-be escapees are shot.

So how did an elderly convict like Ridd – that was the old man's name – manage to escape? It was because he combined forces with an accomplice – a woman named Bel – who, like him, had an outstanding talent. She was an expert in the field of electronics. He was a powerful mind bender.

Ridd had been kept on drugs ever since he became a resident on Four Eighty-One, to stop him from using his mind to cause trouble. In time his mind became immune to the drugs he was taking – but he didn't let on.

The night came when Bel and Ridd, supposedly out for a stroll, came as close to the outport barriers as is permitted for prisoners. The automatic spotlights at Gate Three found them and stayed on them, whilst an amplified electronic voice warned over and over again, "YOU HAVE APPROACHED A PROHIBITED AREA – MOVE AWAY IMMEDIATELY, OR YOU WILL BE FIRED ON." The two criminals moved away. They had noted exactly where they were when the spotlights and voice were activated. Now, just out of reach, they used an electronic probe to bring the spotlight and voice to life again.

They crouched, out of firing range and off camera – activating and re-activating the automatic barrier. The electronic shield was so sophisticated, that only two guards were needed for each shift. From their position in the watchtower, they could see the surrounding area for miles. But they preferred to rely on the bank of screens, which relayed to them all the necessary information. Every exit and entry to the outport was covered.

That night, when the automatic barrier at Gate Three kept playing up, but no intruder appeared on any of the screens, it was decided that one of the guards should investigate in person. Of course that was all Ridd needed. The fact that the guard was heavily armed made no difference to him. As soon as he was near enough, Ridd struck with his ferocious mind and the guard – groaning horribly and clutching at his eyes – fell.

Some time later the other guard came to investigate his colleague's absence. As soon as he came within range, Ridd blew his mind too. Before anyone came along, the two had entered the outport. Anyone who tried to stop them, Ridd blasted mentally. This left Bel free to use her electronic wizardry. Selecting a vehicle that looked set for flight, she broke through dock security and opened the ship's doors.

Because it was ready for space and the ship has been given clearance for lift-off, personnel in ground control were powerless to stop it. They sent up a chaser ship and warned Home Planet that two of their worst criminals were on the loose.

But they weren't heading for Home – they were heading for Earth.

# Chapter Twenty Seven

## RIDD AND BEL

Ridd and Bel had never seen each other until they met on Four Eighty-One. When they met, there was no attraction, one toward the other – no chemistry. They had been in one of the libraries and Ridd was bored with taking in information of the academic kind. He saw Bel and immediately summed her up as a tough cookie. Which she was. Having no scruples, he entered her mind and there perceived her outstanding skill in electronics. He also read her yearning to escape.

From then it was a matter of striking up a conversation, which led to a friendship of sorts, which in turn led to a cool, calculating partnership. Bel was no fool. She was a woman whose lifestyle had left its mark on her face, making her look older than she was. She had no beauty for Ridd to admire. Only brains. With her electronic know-how and his mind bending skills, they might just make a successful break for it. And they did.

They had decided not to return Home. They knew that security would be on the alert. Escaped convicts would be expected to land in some remote location on the planet – and go from there into hiding.

No. The ship – a miracle, even of Home Planet technology – practically flew itself. It just needed to be fed the co-ordinates that would enable it to find Earth. As part of their escape plan, the couple had immersed themselves in Earth studies for months before their break. They knew they could make an easy life for themselves there – so much of Earth life was chaotic and corrupt – and they both had skills which would likely earn them a lot of money. Specifically – criminal skills.

As she checked over the equipment she would be taking down to Earth with her, Bel fixed Ridd with her pale green eyes: "I want to go to Paris. They may not have Home Planet luxury on Earth, but I learnt in my Earth studies, that Paris is the centre of fashion and beauty. It would be good to feel like a woman again."

"Too long in prison clothes, my dear," observed Ridd, casting a disinterested eye over his companion. "Even Paris couldn't sweeten you. I care little where we go, as long as it's summer – and as long as we can get lost. You'll have to learn French."

"I already speak it, *my dear,*" she mimicked. "I have downloaded the most widely used languages on Earth."

"Fine," replied Ridd. "Just make sure we get down safely. We have to destroy this vehicle and submerge its remains, so we're going to have to splashdown."

Later, as they studied a map of Northern Europe, Bel said, "I got hold of some top-secret information that might prove very useful to us. They have sent globeringers down to Earth again. Full of children."

"Home Government still trying to help Earth? Idiots! Wasting Home technology. Nothing will change Earth for the better." His eyes glittered. "And that suits me fine."

Bel sneered. "You miss the point. Do you not see how advantageous it would be for us to possess a globeringer shoe?"

Ridd regarded Bel with his cold smile. "My dear, you really do improve with age! A globeringer would be a gift. We could drive away from any crime we chose to perpetrate – and re-mask. No-one would be able to trace us."

"Not to mention the comfort and convenience – it would be like a travelling home," added Bel smugly.

"A home with its own built-in defence system. I'm beginning to believe we might actually enjoy life on Earth after all." Ridd's eyes gleamed – he was scheming already. "And all we need do is take it from a handful of children!"

"Exactly. According to my sources, one touched down recently near Paris."

"We can trace it. We have a pulse."

\*

In the very early hours of Sunday morning, when it was still pitch dark and a cool wind was sweeping up the English Channel and across Southern England, a UFO was detected descending through the night sky toward the sea.

A Royal Navy vessel out of Portsmouth raced to the spot where its splashdown had been traced on radar. There was no vessel of any kind to be found. Just two elderly people wearing life jackets and treading water, who seemed overjoyed to be rescued.

Bel and Ridd had invented their story to the last detail.

They recognised the type of ship it was and knew that they would now probably end up in England. So once they had been helped aboard the Navy ship, they spoke with a cultured English drawl. They'd had trouble with the engine on their yacht, which had culminated in a fire. In attempting to call for help, they found their radio had been rendered useless by enormous amounts of static and interference. The boat had sunk, and no-one knew where they were. How delighted they were that the Navy had been on hand!

The ship's crew rallied round, seeing to it that they were comfortable and had everything they needed. Later, the captain came to check on their welfare and to find a few things out for himself. He asked if they had seen or heard anything unusual within the past few hours. Bel's pale eyes opened wide as she pretended to be astonished. "So you heard it, too?"

"We traced something unusual on our radar," the captain replied. "It was in exactly the same location as we found you."

Ridd interrupted the man. "Matter of fact, captain, we were asleep at the time. We heard a strange rushing noise – more like a sort of roar really – wasn't it, dear?" He looked at Bel.

Bel added, "Yes, followed by a horrendous splash. We thought a plane had crashed – didn't we, dear?"

Ridd continued. "The boat rocked like billy-o and we dashed up on deck to have a look, see. The sea seemed to be boiling, oh, about half a mile away, but there was absolutely nothing to be seen."

"Nothing," emphasised Bel. "It was at that point that we smelt the burning..."

"Fire in the engine. Thought we'd soon be able to put it out, but it was more serious than we thought. When we realised it was out of control, we tried to call for help...and that's when we found out we'd got a dicky radio... interference... static... couldn't make the damn thing work!"

Captain Harriman treated the elderly couple with extreme courtesy. But he was deeply suspicious. Serving some thirty years in the Navy, he had been in the Falklands and Gulf Wars – and numerous other skirmishes in different parts of the Earth. He was well acquainted with human nature, good and bad. Something very strange had happened during the night and these two were part of it. Their story sounded convincing... but he felt somehow... that they were fakes. Where they were from, he had no idea. He would have given anything to have had a peek inside the waterproof bag which had practically never left the old man's grasp. He had made up his mind that he was going to detain them.

He didn't know that the workings of his mind were wide open to the old man. So when the Captain next glanced at him, he was fixed by the dark, evil glare of Ridd's eyes.

It was in a trance that the captain made arrangements for a launch to take the elderly couple ashore. There, a Navy staff car would be on hand to take them to a hotel, where – Bel told the driver – their son would pick them up and take them home. No questions were asked. The story Bel and Ridd told was accepted as genuine.

Only some two hours later, did Captain Harriman feel the powerful effects of Ridd's mind control ebb away. He felt as if he were coming out of a general anaesthetic.

He remembered the two, but his suspicions had been as good as surgically removed. Even the UFO became just a curious incident worth a mention in the ship's log – but nothing more.

# Chapter Twenty Eight

## TRACING GLOBERINGER FIVE

"We need a cash machine," stated Bel flatly. "We can't pay for this."

They were in the hotel restaurant – open for Sunday breakfast – and had ordered fruit juice and croissants.

"I think that lies within your field of specialities my dear," answered Ridd. "Want to go and look for one?"

Bel got to her feet – and checking she had the right equipment with her – left the premises.

Being Sunday morning there were not many people about. Bel found a cash machine with no difficulty at all. With what appeared to be a lipstick, she rendered its security systems useless. On request, the machine gladly presented her with a thousand pounds – and ceased to work effectively after that. The next person to come along and use it, saw on the screen:-

SSORRY – THISSS MACHINE ISS OUT OUT OUT OF RODER

When Bel returned, Ridd was wearing his cold smile. "I have just used the pulse. There appears to be a globeringer some ten miles north of here."

"Is it on the move?"

"Not at the moment."

"Can we track it – using the road systems here?"

"Yes – and of course, we will. But we need a road map... and we have to er... acquire a vehicle."

"Easy," said Bel.

\*

Later that Sunday morning as the two approached Hollybrook, the pulse gave out clearer, stronger signals. Finally, they located the signal's source at the end of a lane. It was coming from a horsebox in a field. Having established the shoe's location, they turned the car and drove back out of Mulberry Lane. Two minutes later they had left the village behind, and were parking in a lay-by next to a field of stubble. Ridd started to talk of how they were going to take the globeringer, but Bel said, "You may have endless supplies of energy, but I haven't. This is a comfortable car, by Earth standards. Before I do anything else – I am going to sleep." She closed her eyes, lowering her seat until she was almost horizontal.

"Goodnight my dear," said Ridd. Sleep was something he indulged in very little. It seemed so much like a waste of time. Leaving Bel asleep in the car, he strolled back into the village.

By this time, the church bells had started to ring. Ridd sat on a low, stone wall and watched, as village folk went to worship in whatever way they did in this part of Earth. He caught snatches of their thoughts as they passed. Little people – with little thoughts...

Then he caught something far more intense. Distress.

Outrage. Thoughts were pouring out of someone. Someone who was approaching him. The thinker was a boy. His hands were in his pockets, his head bowed. He passed the place where Ridd was sitting, completely preoccupied.

It was like being engulfed by the backwash of a passing ship. Anger...hurt... and not far from the surface – vulnerability. But what caused Ridd to feel a surge of unholy joy, was the fact that the boy was thinking in the Home tongue. The deadly tendrils of his mind reached out...

*

After Ridd thought he had disposed of Brod, he returned to the car. Ridd – who was used to controlling people – making them cringe – was not prepared for the reaction he got from Bel, when he told her what he had done.

Her face turned white. Her pale green eyes blazed, as she said with deadly quietness, "What? You did what?" There was a long pause. Then she snarled, "You despicable smear of dirt! You come to me with a smirk – and tell me you've killed one of the globeringer children! I may have killed a few people in my time – but never, never have I *ever* killed a child!!"

"My dear, how else are we going to get rid of them? You let sentiment get in the way of progress."

"Sentiment? You call it sentiment? Between us, we have the power to do almost anything we like – and you have to resort to killing innocent children? Well, *my dear*," she mocked, "you can manage on your own from now on. Though how you will do that I don't know!

Without my knowledge you may have difficulty sur-viving!"

It was at that point that the horsebox – which they recognised immediately – passed the place where they were parked. A motorbike – which had been following it – took over, its driver signalling for the horsebox to follow. Ridd screwed up his eyes and concentrated – his gaze fixed on the back of the pillion passenger. "That's the boy! He's not dead! The motorbike rider must have..."

"...must have foiled your gutless design!" Bel turned on the ignition and swung the car out into the road. "Let's follow them!" As she drove, Bel said, "If you ever lay a finger on any of those children again – you're on your own. Is that understood?"

Ridd didn't answer. He was trying to read Rob's thoughts. "They have two adults in their group. One of them is human. They are ultimately heading for the laboratory where he works, but they intend to stop off on the way."

"So... we could get there ahead of them. Did you get the name of the place?"

"Ferndean."

# Chapter Twenty Nine

**THE LABORATORY**

Such a lot had happened since Globeringer Five had come through the car wash, that the young mental energists had given very little thought to their individual assignments. Here at the laboratory, Ean would hand in a lengthy, top-secret report about her year on Home Planet. There would be recommendations from Home for the management of Earth's forests. Ean, as a tree specialist and who had learnt the Home tongue, would help to explain and apply those recommendations.

Other Earth scientists, a select few, had exchanged with their counterparts from Home Planet and would have brought back specialist knowledge in their own departments. They would be 'swapping back' just as Ean and Rob were doing.

Now though, the alien children must briefly merge with human society. Observing carefully, they would each select and befriend an Earth twin. At a time just right for it, that twin would receive a unique intellectual/creative gift, delivered by means of a mind-lock. Then the young Home Planet scientists, their mission complete, would return Home.

As they approached the laboratory with its high wire fences, Mab had another surge of homesickness. Planet Earth was so... so far away... and foreign. She missed her family and wondered if the others in her group were suffering too. They had been warned they would feel like this from time to time. She focused again on her assignment. It was clear in her mind. She wanted to be able to get on with it and return – safe.

The shoe turned down a driveway, at the entrance of which was a large notice:-

### PRIVATE PROPERTY
### AUTHORISED PERSONNEL ONLY

"They don't actually say what the place is, do they?" observed Treo.

"Security reasons," stated Rob, who was driving.

"Will they know who we are?" asked Jay.

Ean answered him. "Rob contacted them on the shoe link just before we left Hollybrook. They are expecting us." Then she added thoughtfully, "If people only knew..."

"Knew what?" said Mab, leaning toward Ean.

"That this vehicle is full of aliens. There would be an army and police escort. There'd be helicopters overhead and news reporters fighting one another to take pictures. Television cameras and sound cars would probably block the road..."

"It sounds a tad nerve-wracking," Rob said. He continued, more quietly, "Go easy. You're sounding just a little scary."

"Is that how you think of us, Ean? As *aliens*?" asked Brod. "Well we *are* aliens, aren't we? But we're the super-

148

intelligent, well-meaning type." Then, with a grin, he added, "That is, with the exception of Jay."

Jay made a hideous face and began to grunt.

"Don't knock Jay," said Ean, joining in the laughter. "He's the one who made me better!"

As soon as the man at the laboratory gates saw Rob and Ean, he smiled. "Hello Mrs Farr. Long time, no see! Had a good trip away?"

"Hello Ken! Nice to see you. Yes, it was a good trip."

The barrier was lifted and the camper passed slowly through. They were directed to a parking space surrounded by grass and trees and flower beds. Ean noticed how much better the place was looking since she last saw it and wondered if it was Rob's influence. She saw that they now employed a gardener – an old man was hoeing the flower beds. Before, they had always left it up to the caretakers to run a lawn mower over the grass and the rest was allowed to run wild.

It occurred to Ean, as they walked toward the main building, that for the first time they would be leaving the shoe completely unattended. The thought made her feel distinctly uneasy. She stopped suddenly.

"What?" said Rob.

"The shoe. We can't leave it unattended."

"What d'you think can happen to it, Ean? This is a secure place."

"I don't know. But I'm not happy about leaving it."

"You've been inside it for too long – that's your trouble! It'll be..."

"No Rob..." Brod cut in. "Ean's right. It would be a mistake to leave the shoe."

"What's got into you two? The shoe is safe there. I've sealed it, for goodness sake!"

Brod though, refused to move. He was deathly white, staring at Rob – and Ean knew he was thought speaking. Only, unlike the others, she didn't know what was being said.

*"The gardener, Rob! It's him!"*

*"Are you sure you're not being paranoid after this morning's fright?"*

*"I'm certain. Unseal the shoe, Rob! We have to get out of here! And don't look in his direction!"*

Rob's reaction was to unseal the shoe and say softly – for Ean's benefit – "Get in the shoe everyone. We have to go. Now! Ean, you drive!"

Ean, who had felt all along that something was not right, needed no pushing. Once in the driver's seat, she had the shoe in motion.

Ken, at the gate, saw them coming and looked surprised.

"Lift the barrier Ken!" she mouthed through the windscreen.

Ken tried to lift the barrier but suddenly his face crumpled and he fell forward. Ean was acutely aware of her own vulnerable mind. But Rob and the others were already forming a mental shield, their minds locked protectively round hers. She activated the attack beam and the barrier disintegrated. Roaring through the gateway, the camper disappeared down the driveway and turned onto the main road.

\*

It was in the interests of putting some distance between the laboratory and themselves that Ean broke the speed limit. Normal campers would never clock between eighty and ninety miles per hour. But of course this was not a normal camper, and it went like a rocket. It was only after Ean heard the wail of a police siren that she realised what speed she was doing.

The children were sitting back in their seats. Rob slid into the seat next to Ean and said, "It seems as though we have the police escort you were talking about earlier."

"What's the best thing to do? We can't let them catch us!"

"If you don't want them to catch us, you know what to do!"

"Let's see..." Ean muttered, racking her memory of the area. "I think I know where we can go."

"Somewhere we can disappear and re-mask?" Rob asked.

"Leave it to me!"

The performance of the shoe was such that the police vehicle was soon left way behind. But Ean knew that they would be summoning help and it wouldn't be long before they were heading her off at a crossroads somewhere. They fled the country roads, overtaking and swinging back quickly to avoid oncoming traffic. Ean was grateful it was Sunday and there was less traffic on the road. They were very near to where she wanted to be – a disused airfield with an old hangar – when a second police car, lights flashing, came out of a side turning and screeched to a stop across the road in front of them. Hardly slowing at all, Ean swung violently to the left.

Mounting the verge she swerved round the police car, back onto the road, and accelerated away again.

The airfield was on her left with an old, wooden gate barring the entrance. Once more Ean used the attack beam and the gate, which was flimsy anyway, shattered. As she made for the hangar, she hoped she wouldn't have to destroy any doors to get into it. Rob turned the runway surface to ice as they careered through the open hangar doors. Seconds later the camper was glowing with rainbow colours.

As the police cars – by now there were three of them – waltzed and skidded out of control on the ice outside, Brod broke the silence inside the shoe. "Of course, if we punch a hole in the far wall, they might think we've driven through – and give chase..."

"No sooner said than done!" Rob blasted the far wall where the seams were already coming apart.

"Er, it's metal. You melted it," said Brod.

"Add some effects!" suggested Mab.

"Will you guys stop breathing down my neck!" snarled Rob, making some changes to his handiwork.

"I don't think they'll believe a little old camper did that!" Ean said, surveying the twisted metal.

"They'll have to – there's no other explanation is there?"

"No," said Ean.

The occupants of what was now a helicopter kept their heads low and watched through the spy plate as several members of Her Majesty's police force checked over the hangar. The runway had been de-iced as soon as they saw the police abandon their cars. The breach in the end wall had been discovered and the chase was taken up again in a different direction. Of course they believed they were searching for a very badly damaged vehicle, and wondered how on earth it had got so clean away...

# Chapter Thirty

## STACEY'S VISITOR

"Of course you realise that, having unsuccessfully attempted to kill one of those children, you have revealed our presence!" Bel had observed icily, as they'd arrived at Ferndean – well ahead of the camper/globeringer. "They may not know exactly where we are, but they know we are in the area – and they will now be watching out for us!"

Ridd had sighed. He knew he could never have managed to escape to Earth without Bel, but the woman was beginning to seriously irritate him.

Matters were not improved when later, true to Bel's prediction, his presence at Ferndean was detected and the shoe driven away at break-neck speed to a place of safety. Now what were they going to do?

"It's no good being angry, my dear. What I've done – I've done. So they know of our presence – but we can still outwit them."

"Tell me how we're going to do that – they're always going to be one step ahead of us!"

"There are other ways... "

"Such as?" snapped Bel. Then she turned her head slightly as her ears caught the sound of the police siren.

Ridd heard it too – and smiled. "My dear, it seems as though they have brought trouble upon themselves, with such a hasty departure!"

"Huh! The police won't catch a globeringer..."

"Yes, but they may be occupied for a while, shaking them off." He became thoughtful.

Bel let him think. She had never been tempted to enter the catacombs of Ridd's mind.

Finally he said, "This is a good time to return to the woman's house. There may be members of her family I can... manipulate."

Bel's eyes gleamed. "I'll leave it in your capable hands – or should I say 'mind'? You'd better take the car – I'll see if I can er.... find another one!" Then, clutching his arm until her long finger nails bit into his flesh, she added, "If there are any children, go easy – d'you hear? There is plenty you can do without hurting them."

"Leave it to me, my dear...." he replied, already planning how he could use a vulnerable member of the woman's family to assist him in hijacking the globeringer.

Ridd knew that with the pulse, he would easily locate the shoe again. It would no doubt re-mask and return to a location near the woman's house. He had been near enough to the shoe and its occupants to read each of their minds. She was the human – the one who thought in the English language. It was her house, next to the field in which the horsebox had parked. Before he set off, it was agreed that Bel would remain in Ferndean until after dark. Their business there was by no means finished.

\*

Stacey was at home alone with the kitten when the old man knocked on the front door. Her dad had taken Jon to the Sunday afternoon football match. She was happy to stay in and wait for Miss Wilson, who had phoned back to say she would pick the kitten up during the afternoon. In fact she thought the knock on the door *was* Miss Wilson.

"Hello Stacey." On her doorstep a bearded old man with dark – almost black – eyes, was smiling at her.

Stacey stared back at him. "Who are you?"

"I am a friend of your mother. Can I come in?"

Stacey continued to stare at him. She remembered Rob at yesterday's fete, who said he knew her mum. She'd felt differently about him, trusted him somehow. Now here was someone else claiming to know her mum. But as she returned the old man's gaze – she felt spooked. She certainly didn't trust *this* one. "No you can't come in!"

"Oh, don't be like that!" he laughed, without sounding amused. "You see, I know where your mother is."

"Where?" demanded Stacey.

"Well if you invite me in, I shall be able to tell you."

Against all her better instincts, Stacey stepped back and the old man entered the house, following Stacey into the kitchen-diner, where the kitten was curled up on its favourite chair.

"What a beautiful little cat. Is it yours?" he said, bending towards it. The kitten opened its eyes wide and was immediately on all four paws with its back arched. Its fur stood on end as it hissed and spat.

"It doesn't like you," said Stacey smugly, thinking what a sensible kitten it was.

"Never mind!"

"You said you would tell me where my mother was if I invited you in."

"So I did. It's a long story, though. She's been much further away from home than you could possibly imagine. My dear, would you allow me a glass of water – I'm very thirsty."

Stacey ran a glass of water and handed it over. "I know she's been far away and I know she's been in danger. But where is she now? And is she safe?"

"She is not at all far from here. I have just come from where she was. But whether she is safe or not is entirely up to you."

"How could it be up to me? I haven't seen her for a year!" Stacey's temper began to flare. "For goodness sake, can't you just tell me where she is, and stop being all stupid and mysterious!"

"Don't you call me stupid! I came here to help you, you rude little girl." He sighed – Earthlings! All full of sentimental rubbish!

Stacey folded her arms across her chest and glared at the man, although she found it difficult. The man had very strange eyes.

"OK, OK!" he said. "Let's make this easier! Just close your eyes for a moment, Stacey. I can show you better that way."

Stacey didn't want to, but found she couldn't help closing her eyes.

"Sit down, my dear..." The voice had become cold.

Stacey sat down. Her head was filled with blue, the soft blue of a summer sky. She saw clouds, and knew that indeed it was the sky. There came to her ears the distant clatter of a helicopter's rotor blades and moments later a large yellow helicopter flew across her mind.

"Now then, can you guess who is inside that?"

"My mum?" said Stacey, much more quietly.

"That's right, your mum. Now just watch this..."

The whirling blades on the chopper began to falter. The whole thing began to tip – and it was obvious that it was going to crash. Stacey's hands flew to her face.

"OH NO! OH *NO*!"

Suddenly the chopper righted itself and the blades began to turn normally again. Stacey tried to open her eyes but couldn't.

"I did that Stacey. You ask me if your mum is safe. Watch again..."

The chopper's tail began to spin round and gradually it began to lose height.

"DON'T! *DON'T*!" she cried.

The spinning stopped, the chopper regained height and flew on normally once more.

"Shall I show you again?" came the voice.

"YOU *PIG*! WHAT ARE YOU DOING? WHO ARE YOU? WHY DID YOU COME HERE?"

"Ah! I was thinking you would never ask! Open your eyes, Stacey."

Stacey opened her eyes.

"That helicopter is not what it seems." His voice had an intense quietness about it. "It is, in fact, a space vehicle. It is a wonderful piece of alien technology. It can change its outward appearance so that it looks like anything that is familiar to Earth people. At the moment it is an aircraft – but it could change at the wish of those driving it – into a car, train, bus, shed..." He leant closer to her. "*Horsebox*!"

Stacey decided that the man was a complete nutter – and was terrified.

"You remember the horsebox that was parked across the road last night? The one that later drove into the field and parked next to your garden?"

"Yes... I... I think so." Stacey was wishing that Miss Wilson would arrive, or her dad and Jon would come home. Agitated, she became preoccupied with smoothing her hair away from her face, as she tried to think of ways she could outwit her ghastly visitor.

"Well, it was there for the express purpose of bringing your mother home. Home from another planet! Your mother has been on another planet Stacey!"

"*You're* on another planet!" cried Stacey. She jumped to her feet, grabbed the edge of the rug on which the old man was standing, and pulled hard. As he crashed to the ground, she ran from the house and out into the sunshine, looking for someone who could help her. There was no-one nearby. She ran down Mulberry Lane – she could see Gaynor's Derek mowing his front lawn. He was stripped to the waist and had a body full of tattoos. There was a rag tied round his head as a sweat band. To Stacey he was a reassuring sight. If anyone knew how to deal with the old man, it would be Gaynor's Derek.

But well before she reached Derek's gate she heard a sound which stopped her in her tracks. It was the sound of an approaching helicopter.

She knew it was the yellow helicopter she had been made to see in her mind. Lifting her eyes, she saw that it was heading in her direction from the other side of the village. Stacey turned round. The old man had left the house and was coming slowly towards her.

His face was screwed up – with pain or anger – Stacey didn't know, probably both.

"You know what I can do to that machine up there?" he growled. "I can destroy it!"

Stacey shook her head, crying fresh tears.

The old man jabbed a finger at her. "You think I'm out of my mind, but watch!"

The chopper's engine began to stutter. It lost height.

"NO! NO! NO!" yelled Stacey. Turning to the old man she begged, "Why do you keep doing this? What d'you want me to do?"

He gazed upward and the chopper became stable again. "Sometime after the helicopter lands, it will re-mask. It will change shape. You don't believe me because you are a stupid, narrow minded Earth child. I want you to find out where it lands. Keep track of it but keep out of sight. They won't change its shape if they think anyone is watching, and for that reason they may not change until after dark. When it has changed – after it has changed – you must find out where it goes."

"How can I find out where it goes? It might go too far away for me to find it!" Stacey still believed him to be completely mad.

"It'll be easy. Because it is carrying your mother, it will land not far from here. Then, when it has changed form – it will park next to your house, to make it easy for her to return home. Because you saw it change shape though, you will know that it really *is* an alien space vehicle."

"Yeah..." Stacey said, humouring him. Then suddenly remembering something, she demanded "If the horsebox parked in the field next to my house had my mother in it, why didn't she come home then?"

"I don't know, my dear. They must have forgotten that first they needed to report to her work place near here."

"Is this er, space vehicle, full of aliens then?"

"There are five of them – and your mother."

"I see."

"No you don't see. I want the globeringer! You have to knock on the vehicle door and make them all come out. Invite them into your home. I need you to get them out of the way, so that I can take it."

Stacey imagined herself inviting little grey people with huge black eyes, into her home for a cup of tea and a chat. "And when you have stolen their vehicle? How will they get home?"

"There are other means. There's a mother ship standing just outside Earth's atmosphere. It will send another globeringer to pick them up."

"What if I don't agree to do as you say? It might take ages for this thing to change shape. My dad will wonder where I am!"

"That's too bad. You must follow the globeringer and watch it very closely. I don't care how you do it, but you must get everyone out. I want it empty! Do you understand? If you try to get out of doing it, if you try to call for help, if you do anything to stop me from getting hold of it – I will kill your mother."

Stacey felt a sudden surge of fury. "You are an evil man!" she raged at him. "If you hurt my mother, I'll kill you!"

"Calm yourself, you silly child. Do as you're told – and your mother will remain unharmed!"

Just then a car drew up outside her house and the old

man stared with narrowed eyes as Miss Wilson got out. "Who's that?"

"She's my teacher. She's come to collect her kitten." Stacey made a move to go and meet Miss Wilson.

"Wait! She might prove useful to me. Introduce me to her as... let's see... your grandfather, and then keep your mouth shut."

Stacey approached Miss Wilson, and introduced as her grandfather the last person on Earth she would want to be related to.

Miss Wilson shook hands politely. "Stacey, are you alright? You look as though you've been crying!"

Stacey kept her mouth shut.

"She's not very well er... Miss... er..."

"Wilson. Stacey, wouldn't you be better in bed if you're not well? Maybe it's too hot for you out here!"

"Well now, that's just what I was trying to encourage her to do. To come inside, have a cool drink and lie down." The old man put an affectionate arm round Stacey's shoulders.

Stacey's skin crawled. She felt as though a damp reptile had crawled across her back.

"A good idea!" Miss Wilson smiled brightly at him.

"Stacey tells me the little cat belongs to you. Do please come in and collect it." He walked up the garden path.

Stacey and Miss Wilson followed him into the kitchen-diner.

Remembering its reaction last time he went near it, he instructed Stacey to hand over the kitten.

Miss Wilson was all gratitude. "I'm so relieved she's unharmed! I thought she might have been run over or attacked by another animal!"

Stacey could have told quite a story at that point – but she still kept her mouth shut.

Miss Wilson cradled the kitten in her arms, tickling its tummy. "I've got a special box in the car that she can travel in. Once more, thank you both so much for looking after her. Thank you Stacey – and Stacey's Grandf...." As she caught the old man's eye to smile her thanks at him, she froze.

With the old man bending her mind, Miss Wilson suddenly thought how nice it would be to take Stacey back home with her. The little girl was on her own for the afternoon – and quite clearly at a loose end. Miss Wilson lived on a farm with her parents. She could show Stacey round, and then maybe she would like to have tea with the family. But of course, she must make it right with Stacey's dad. She rummaged in her bag for her mobile phone. "What's your father's mobile phone number, Stacey?"

Stacey was aware that the old man was causing Miss Wilson to think, say and do things beyond her control, but she hadn't a clue what was going on in her teacher's mind. Her dad's mobile phone number she knew by heart, but why should Miss Wilson want to ring him? She was taken aback when the old man promptly gave out the correct number. How did he find that out, for goodness sake?

"My dear, it was quite simple," he said, as Miss Wilson made the call. "The number was in your mind. I just er.... helped myself."

In a trance, Miss Wilson had a friendly conversation with her dad, in which she arranged to take Stacey home for tea and to look around her parents' farm. At first Stacey thought it was real – and started to smile – it sounded like fun!

"No, you stupid girl!" the old man sneered – and the smile vanished from Stacey's face. "I only want your father to *think* you're with your teacher!"

As she carried the kitten to her car and put it in the box on the back seat, Miss Wilson had the last few minutes wiped cleanly from her memory. She drove away, hoping that Stacey would be well enough for school the next day. "Nice girl... " she was thinking, "...sensitive – rather lonely." Maybe she should invite Stacey and some of the students from her year to the farm sometime. They could look around... have some tea...

Stacey stood at the gate with the old man's arm round her shoulder, waving Miss Wilson goodbye. As soon as the car turned into the High Street she quickly shrugged his arm off her shoulder with a scowl and took some steps away from him.

He was smiling his cold smile as he said, "At least your father won't wonder where you are now, Stacey. Can't have him calling the police, can we?" He raised his head, almost as if he was sniffing the wind. "The helicopter... landed... in that direction!" pointing down the lane, past the horse field. He walked away in the opposite direction, and then paused. "Just for the record my dear, I am not a complete nutter. And.... I shall never be far away from you."

And he was gone.

# Chapter Thirty One

**THE RAINBOW EFFECT**

From somewhere up a tree, Stacey had plenty of leaf cover and a good view of the helicopter. It had been easy to find, having chosen to land about three fields away from her house. A couple of walkers out for a Sunday afternoon ramble had stopped to watch it land, and a boy on a bike hung around for a while. Its blades were rotating slowly to a stop, but as there was no further movement from the aircraft – no-one getting out – the spectators gradually moved away.

Except for Stacey.

Finally a man clambered out and Stacey smothered an exclamation. It was Rob, whom she had met at the village fete. That might well mean her mum was on board. Which made Stacey feel uneasy, because it meant that at least part of what the old man had said was true. The field was one of the smallest in the area, with trees surrounding it on three sides. On the far side the land sloped away up a hill. It was as private a spot as you could get in the open countryside around here. Stacey was tempted to run towards the helicopter shouting, "Mum! mum!" but the old man had said that he would never be far away and that thought stopped her. After a while, some young people emerged, followed by a woman. And yes, it was mum!

Stacey whispered to herself, "That's my mum!" watching her smile at the children but noticing also how often she frowned. She thought she understood. So near and yet so far. Mum must be conscious of being close to home – and yet not quite there. Why ever did they have to hang back? What on earth was it that they still had to do, so that she wasn't allowed home yet? Stacey hated the children immediately. They had her mum looking after them, when she should be looking after her – and Jonathan and dad. Who were they anyway? And where were they from?

Whilst the kids in the field played a ball game, Stacey changed her position. She was bored and uncomfortable and found a fairly solid position with her back to the trunk. There was a branch slightly lower down on which she could rest her feet. That was better, a bit more comfortable. She sighed. This was absolutely ridiculous. How long was she going to have to wait, for goodness sake? She leant her head back on the trunk and sighed again...

Nearly falling out of the tree was what woke her up. It was almost dark – and much cooler. The helicopter was just a shape. Its occupants must have gone back inside. Stacey suddenly felt lonely and scared. She peered through the leaves. Why would anybody want to sit in a chopper for hours on end? They must be mad. Then she thought of the mad old man who had sent her on this errand and shuddered. He would never be far away, he had said. The thought of him somewhere near in the darkness made the hairs on the back of her neck stand up. She tried to shut him out of her mind, gazing at the dark shape in the field below.

She sat bolt upright as she suddenly saw what seemed like a strip of purple flame flicker over it. What now? Was there an electrical fault? A fire? But the purple was followed by a luminous blue, then vibrant green which was chased by brilliant yellow... orange... red. The whole machine was glowing, pulsating with gorgeous rainbow colours which became brighter as she stared. It was beautiful. Beautiful! Underneath the rainbow, something was happening. The helicopter was changing shape. It seemed to be melting.... dissolving.... re-forming. The air was alive with static. Stacey's ears popped. Her eyes watered.

Then it hit her. Her mum was in there! How could she have lived through that? As Stacey scrambled down from the tree, scraping her shins and hands, all she could think of was her mum. She must surely be dead. Melted inside that... that.

She was shrieking "Mum! mum!" as she ran across the field. The light show was dimming, the colours dying. An occasional bright glimmer would repeat itself – blue here, green there, until finally it stopped. Stacey stopped too. Now that the light had gone, it was pitch black and she could no longer see where she was going.

She had to stand for a while, waiting for her eyes to get accustomed to the dark. Then it became quite clear that what stood in front of her was not a helicopter at all but a large caravan. Utterly overwhelmed, she thought she was going to faint. But there was something she had to do. What was it? Stumbling forward, whimpering, she didn't realise that she had been heard from inside the shoe.

The door was opened slowly, and standing there in the light from the doorway, completely unharmed, was her mum.

# Chapter Thirty Two

**ALIENS**

Ean jumped down the caravan steps and ran the few short yards to meet her. "Stacey!" she cried, throwing her arms round her daughter. "Darling, what on earth are you doing out here?"

Stacey was trying to talk, but she was sobbing so much that she couldn't get out what she wanted to say.

"She needs help!" called Ean, keeping her arms wrapped round her and walking her towards the caravan.

Rob came to the other side of Stacey. "Come on m'girl. Let's get you inside..."

She was brought into a bright, clean interior which looked nothing like the inside of a caravan at all. There was a soft, comfortable seat for her.

Jay brought her a warm drink and crouched down, putting a hand gently to her dirty face. "Drink, Stacey."

Stacey drank something that tasted strange but soothing and pleasant. Her mum bathed her face while Mab and Treo got to work on her cut legs. When they had done that, they made sure she had finished her drink and started to bathe her hands. Then Jay gave her what looked like a small, fragrant pillow. "Just hold that – and relax..."

Stacey recognised the smell. She glanced up at Jay

with surprise. "This smells just like something I've got growing in my garden!"

"They're healing leaves, Stacey," Jay replied, with an impish smile.

Brushing strands of damp hair from Stacey's face, her mum said lovingly, "I don't think you could have had your hair cut since I went away – it's grown so long! And you've grown..." She gave Stacey another big hug. "I have missed you so much!"

"Where have you *been* mum... it's been so... so... awful without you... and dad misses you, and so does Jonathan... we've tried to get used to it, but..." She glared fiercely at her mum. "Now you're home you're not going away again – are you?"

"Stacey – I'm home for good! But how did you get yourself in such a state, darling?"

"I was up a tree, watching you. I saw the helicopter land. How did you do that... that...?"

All four children were gazing at her now. Rob said quietly to Ean, "She saw us re-mask."

"So it's true then?" Stacey moaned. "What the old man said was true..."

At the words 'old man', the children's eyes widened. They stared first at Rob, then at Ean. Brod came over from the spy plate.

He had a long, serious face, not as cute as the other one, Stacey decided.

"What did he look like?"

"Horrible. Old, with a beard and dark eyes like... like.. black holes. He told me you were aliens, but you're not aliens are you? You're normal human beings."

There was complete silence. Stacey began to feel peculiar, as if she were in a dream.

"Mum – he said you had been to another planet."

The silence continued. Stacey covered her face with her hands. Then she took her hands away and looked at each of the children one by one. The dream-like feeling continued. Finally she said in a small voice, "Well... if you *are* aliens, you're all very nice." Then she added sadly, "And my hair's such a mess!"

*

She was questioned closely by her mum and Rob about the old man's visit. When they asked her if she knew why he had come, she felt she could only tell them so much. "Er... I don't really know," she replied lamely.

"What did he say? What did he do?" Her mum persisted. "It's very important that you tell us, Stacey."

"He made me close my eyes and then he showed me the helicopter – it was in the air. I knew you were in it, mum. Then he told me to watch, and he seemed to be able to make it go wrong, so that it looked as if it was going to crash. He did it twice." Stacey's face was very pale as she remembered. "I thought it was just a kind of dream – but I was really scared. Then I pulled the mat out from under him and ran out of the house."

"Oh dear. And did he come after you?"

"Yes. I saw Derek – you know, Gaynor's Derek – mowing his front lawn, and I was about to yell for help when I heard the helicopter. I knew it was the one I had seen in my mind. And it was. The old man got near to me and told me he had the power to destroy it and as I watched, the engine seemed to go wrong and it looked as if it might crash..." Stacey bit her lip.

Rob and her Mum exchanged meaningful glances. Mum said, "I did suffer a momentary mental blackout, just as we were flying over Mulberry Lane. Rob was about to take over the controls when I suddenly came to, and stabilised the machine again."

Stacey was too involved in the retelling of events to wonder at her mum flying a helicopter. She continued: "I yelled at him to stop it. Why was he doing such a terrible thing? And then... and then..."

"...And then he told you what he wanted you to do for him," finished her mum.

Wretchedly aware of the old man's threat, Stacey shut her mouth tight and studied her feet. "I can't tell you any more."

"He threatened to kill your mum," Rob stated with sympathy. "If you didn't somehow get us all out of the globeringer – perhaps by inviting us into your home – thus leaving it free for him to steal it."

"How did you know that?" gasped Stacey.

Her mum put a warm hand on her arm. "He read your mind, sweetheart. It is far better for us to know the truth. The old man is evil and very powerful, but we have the ability to fight him."

"And he is not going to kill your mum!"

"But he nearly made your helicopter crash!"

"That's true!" admitted Rob. "But we were unaware that he was almost directly below us. We let our guard down. We won't do it again!"

# Chapter Thirty Three

## QUESTIONS

Stacey was shown the bathroom at the back of the shoe and had the best shower of her life, water jetting at her from vents in the walls and ceiling. When the water switched off, as if it knew she was clean, warm air flowed gently through the same vents. Then came a fine mist of fragrant lotion, conditioning her skin and her hair.

Mum handed her clothes in to her and she emerged fully dressed.

Next, she sat on the floor with her back against her mum's legs and had her hair brushed. This was something mum always used to do. Even when Stacey was old enough to brush her own hair thoroughly, she would sit on the floor at home and mum would perform this loving luxury. Long, firm strokes of the brush...

Suddenly Stacey put her hands up and brought them down hard onto the brush, stopping the motion of her mum's hands.

"What is it, Stacey?"

"I've just realised... you didn't answer any of my questions!" She scrambled to her feet and turned, staring at her mum accusingly. "I asked you where you'd been, and you didn't tell me. I asked you if you'd been on another planet and you said nothing!" Stacey's temper was rising – the volcano was rumbling. "I don't want you to touch me again until you have explained why you left us so suddenly, without an explanation – and why you were gone for so long!"

Ean sat with the brush in her hand, gazing back at her daughter. Her eyes were dark with guilt, shock, all sorts of emotions.

"...AND YOU HAVEN'T EVEN SAID YOU WERE *SORRY!!*" Stacey yelled. The volcano had erupted.

Rob got to his feet. He put out an unspoken command: *"OK you guys, let's give Ean and her daughter some space!"* All four got to their feet and moved to other end of the shoe. Rob put his hand toward the ceiling and a screen descended silently, shutting them off.

Stacey was still yelling. "YOU SAT THERE, BRUSHING MY HAIR, AS IF NOTHING HAD CHANGED! BUT EVERYTHING HAS CHANGED! I DON'T EVEN KNOW YOU! THE MUM I KNEW WOULD NEVER HAVE GONE OFF AND LEFT HER HUSBAND AND KIDS WITHOUT A WORD!"

"I'm sorry," Ean said quietly, as if trying out the words to see how they sounded.

Naturally Stacey didn't hear. "AND WHO IS *EAN,* FOR GOODNESS SAKE?!"

"I'm sorry, Stacey," Ean repeated, more loudly, and then as Stacey seemed to subside a little, she said it again. "I'm sorry!"

"It was a year mum – a whole *year!* We needed you. Where *were* you?"

"STACEY! I'M *SORRY!* Are you going to calm down and listen to me? Do you really want to know where I've been and why I went?"

"Yes."

Ean handed Stacey the hairbrush. "You'd better carry on brushing your hair if you don't want me to touch you. You don't want it to dry frizzy, do you?"

And while Stacey brushed her hair, her mum began her story. "Stacey, we live on a beautiful planet. It is just full of life and movement and colour. Think of some of the places you have seen on TV. Think of the varieties of wildlife, think of the people."

To Stacey's amazement, the screen which had descended between them and Rob and the children suddenly came alive with coloured pictures, as if it were a giant television. A great African plain spread out before her, dotted with strange shaped trees which stood starkly against a vivid blue sky. Moving in towards one of the trees, Stacey saw a leopard spread along one of the branches, its rich coat dappled with sunlight. It stared at Stacey with its amber eyes, swishing its tail. Stacey could smell the warm fur and the strange pungent scent of cat. She could hear it purr. The leopard descended from the tree, walked off the screen, came into the room – and disappeared. Stacey had become rigid with fear, but her mum whispered, "It's OK, it's not real. It only looks it."

The sun was going down behind the African plain. The sky was glowing pink and orange, then it deepened to purple. The trees were like figures on a tapestry. A long-necked bird flew across the dying sun – and the picture changed. A million diamonds shimmered on a sunlit sea. Stacey could just make out the misty blue out-line of some distant land. She knew something was about to happen – and it did. A pod of killer whales broke the surface, glistening stark black and white. One of them had a calf leaping at her side. They followed the whales under the sea and the calf swam away from its parent, out of the picture, vanishing before swooping right into Stacey's face.

Next, her eyes were filled with the majesty of snow capped mountains. She could just make out an eagle, hovering on the wind. They panned down the slopes, through the forest, trailing a mighty river in its descent. Here, salmon leapt, and huge brown bears prowled. The sound of rushing water filled Stacey's ears. She could feel the cold sting of its spray on her face, the scent of pine in her nostrils.

She became spectator to every kind of scene. Warm coral seas, frozen windswept glaciers, great parched deserts, lush green jungles. It was rather like a nature programme and she was about to say as much to her mum, demanding what this had to do with her absence for year, when suddenly the picture made her feel as though she were lifting off from the ground, she was drifting above the leafy canopy of a tropical forest. Higher she rose, until underneath her the expanse of trees spread out like a great green carpet. Now she could see rivers and the edge of the land shelving into the sea, far, far below. Continents took on shapes she would normally identify in a school atlas. The curve of the Earth fell away beneath her and a beautiful blue globe filled her vision – hanging in the blackness of space.

At first she thought it was the sea she could hear, pounding some distant shore. But as she listened, it resolved itself. It was the sound of breathing. It wasn't the deep, even breathing that comes when someone is asleep. It was as if someone was gasping after a long uphill climb. Stacey glanced questioningly at her mum.

"It's the Earth, Stacey."

"But the Earth doesn't breathe!"

# Chapter Thirty Four

## PHOTOSYNTHESIS

"Oh yes it does!"

The breathing had become slower, more laboured.

"And do you know what has always acted as its lungs...? Its forests and jungles, Stacey. The great, rolling expanses of dense greenery. Because of the process called photosynthesis..."

"You've told me about it. Something to do with green plants giving out oxygen..."

"That's right. Of course photosynthesis occurs in every green plant: the grass at your feet, the fern on your window sill, shrubs on the patio, as well as forests full of trees. Fuelled by sunlight, green plants use carbon dioxide, water and minerals to produce food, directly or indirectly, for almost all life on Earth. And in the process, they replenish the atmosphere, removing carbon dioxide and releasing pure oxygen."

Stacey sighed. Nothing had changed. Mum was rattling on about the environment just as she always had. But it was so good to have her back. She tried hard to concentrate.

"Photosynthesis is an incredibly complex operation.

If humans were to even *try* and imitate the process, they would have to build enormous factories, no doubt equipped with tons of noisy, smelly machinery – and staffed with hundreds of scientists, all demanding spectacular wages! But, Stacey, these microscopic 'machines' perform at thousands, or even millions of cycles a second. They are solar powered. There is no noise, pollution, or ugliness. All you have is a wonderful variety of green plants which give us food, comfort and shelter – and which purify the atmosphere... "

"Mum ... " Stacey had done her best to listen, but she was growing impatient. "You already knew all this. You didn't have to visit another planet to find out!"

"Patience, Stacey – I'm coming to it! You are also aware – because we've talked about it, and it's a well documented fact – that the areas in which the most dense greenery occurs, is being systematically destroyed."

"The tropical rain forests."

"You've heard all the statistics Stacey. An area greater than the size of England is burned or felled every year, and so on. But much of the slashing and burning is done by poor people who are clearing the forest from around their homes in order to try and make a living from the soil. What you have to understand, is that the soil from which these forests grow is very poor, the people can only use it for two or three years' farming, before it becomes exhausted. So then, of course, they slash and burn another plot, which will last them for another two or three years, before they clear yet another patch. They have to survive, but they are destroying the very ecosystem on which they depend. It's a vicious circle..."

179

"But how can the soil be so poor?" Stacey wanted to know, "when it's got all those trees and vines and stuff, growing out of it?"

"Surprising, isn't it? The topsoil in an ordinary temperate forest may be as much as seven feet deep. But the topsoil in a rain forest is rarely deeper than two inches!"

"That *can't* be right, mum!"

"Bear with me, my love. The forest is not dependent on its soil. It literally feeds on itself. Most of the nutrients needed by the plants and trees are supplied by branch and leaf litter which covers the forest floor. Because it's so hot and humid they are decomposed quickly – by termites, fungi and other organisms. Nothing is wasted Stacey. Everything is recycled. Through transpiration and evaporation from the forest canopy, the rain forest even recycles three quarters of the rainfall it receives. Later, the clouds formed by this process water the forest again. But this wonderful, self-sustaining system is becoming exhausted. The worst culprits of course, are not the small farmers, but what they call 'agri-businesses' – huge mining and logging industries – and hydro-electric dam projects. Cut down a small area of rain forest and within a few years it will restore itself, but level a large area and it may never recover. The heavy rain washes away the nutrients, and the hot sun bakes the thin layer of topsoil until finally only coarse grass can grow. Now, on Home Planet..."

"At last, she's gonna explain to me!" Stacey sighed.

Her mum laughed. The atmosphere lightened. "On Home Planet, they have ways of managing their ecology – we can learn so much from them. Especially by *seeing* what they do!"

180

And Ean went on to speak of the way Home Planet dwellers had, since their earliest beginnings, treated their environment with respect. Knowing that the soil on which they dwelt was immeasurably older than they were, they 'listened' to it, even as they secured a living from it. They observed how its qualities changed from place to place and treated it accordingly. Ean gave examples as to how, for instance, farmers planted their trees in layers. Small, medium and large trees in ranks, which, as they grew, had the effect of making their farms look like natural forests.

They had developed the famous *folia prophylaxis beautifica* from years of careful research. Combining the characteristics of the strongest, most luxuriant, fastest growing plants, healing leaves had taken on a life of their own, enriching the soil wherever they were planted, scenting and purifying the air with delightful fragrance – and yielding in those leaves a cure for most ills.

When Rob came to work at Ferndean, he had been trying to help the scientists there to develop an Earth equivalent of healing leaves. Planted and nurtured with special Home Planet expertise, such growth would greatly advance the greening of the damaged forests of Earth. It would combat soil degradation and allow the small farming communities to use the same plot for many years. It would also reforest the great tracts laid waste by the big businesses.

After working at Ferndean for some weeks, Rob had been told by his watch captain that if he hadn't already done so, he should perform his mind-lock with his selected 'Earth twin' and leave. Time was running out. Even well integrated aliens were reminded that they'd had ample time to complete their assignments. But as Rob had locked minds with Elizabeth Farr, she'd woken up. And not just from the strange sleep that enfolded her. She had woken up – completely aware and convinced as to his strange identity.

The hairbrush in Stacey's hand had long ceased to brush. It now lay idle in her lap as she sat cross-legged on the floor and listened to what happened on that decisive day a year ago.

*

"Where are you *really* from?" Elizabeth demanded. They had just eaten lunch and were relaxing in the laboratory's rest room. And when Rob hadn't answered because he couldn't, she had stated, "You're not from this planet."

He'd touched a tiny button on his watch and had pointed it to the ceiling. What had appeared above her head was an astronomical chart. Starting at Earth's solar system, a light blue line had stretched out, and as the chart changed, it had travelled away and away across the light years until it reached the star system where Home Planet was located.

"How did you know?" Rob had watched her carefully.

"The way you are able – unerringly – to read my mind, Rob. The way you have brought our research ahead by leaps and bounds. This is no experiment to you –you've done it all before. You never make a mistake. You always know exactly what to do next and just how it should be done. Since you've been with us Rob, we've never taken a backward step. Are you surprised I'm gutted at your leaving?"

This had caused Rob to think for a long time and Elizabeth had wished *she* could read *his* mind. Finally he'd said calmly, "Why don't you go in my place?"

Elizabeth had just stared back at him – her face wearing a 'you must be joking' expression.

"Liz, you could do it. Our planet is the same as yours. We have the same physiology – the same physical make-up. It's just that I'm homan and you're human! Home technology makes the trip easy. For you, it would be just like taking a long train journey..."

At this Liz had burst out laughing.

Rob leaned forward and produced another argument. "Liz, other scientists from Earth are going. There's a marine biologist from California, an astrophysicist from Russia, a German doctor of ... "

"So your presence here on Earth is known?"

"Not officially. We don't wish to be investigated by the governments, military forces and space agencies of Earth. The merest few are aware – those who have the ecological interests of the planet at heart."

"How long will these scientists be gone for?"

"A year."

"That's a long time, Rob."

"Think of it as a field trip, Liz. You would gain immensely valuable experience, if you worked alongside our people for a year. The knowledge you bring back with you could help change the future of Earth's environment."

Liz's face wore the most serious expression Rob had ever seen. She'd turned to gaze out of the window.

"But a *year!*" she whispered.

"Isn't it true though, that people's jobs often take them away from home and family? Sometimes as much as two years at a time?" Rob reasoned. "If you exchange with me, it means I also am away from Home for a year. Of course I have no life-partner, no children, so maybe it's not quite so hard for me – although I should miss Home!"

"How should I explain a year's absence to Peter and the children?" Liz bit her lip – and Rob had smiled, knowing she would accept the challenge.

\*

There was silence inside the shoe.

The screen still depicted Earth, but as her mum had been explaining things, it had changed. The planet had become shrouded in grey, choking cloud. Stacey could hear the breathing once more, and found it distressing to listen to. It was rasping, as if every intake of breath was a huge effort. But as she watched, the picture faded, the sound of the breathing stopped and – as the silence continued – the screen lifted and disappeared into the ceiling.

The children were trying very hard to appear occupied, concentrating hard on the writing of their journals. Then one by one, they lifted their faces and gazed anxiously at Stacey. Rob spoke softly on their behalf. "Has that helped answer your questions?"

"Yes," Stacey answered. "It was horrible, but I understand now why she went."

Rob's eyes were serious but kind. "Good girl. And she's home now, Stacey – with information in her head that could help save Earth from dying."

Treo had been chewing the end of her writing stick but took it out of her mouth to say, "Cool. "

Stacey flicked a look at her mum – a mixture of embarrassment and respect.

"And *who* is Ean?" Her eyes went back to Rob.

"Simply a shortened form of your mum's name – Elizabeth Anne. It was our special assignment name for her. Suits her, don't you think?" He rose and took his seat at the control panel. "And now, if we are to play into the hands of our nasty friend out there, I'd better drive this thing down the lane and park it in the field next to your house."

"Yes, and you can all come in and have supper!"

## Chapter Thirty Five

**FIRE AT FERNDEAN**

Bel thought it was likely that the laboratory at Ferndean would be permanently staffed – and permanently guarded. She reckoned it must be one of the few places on the planet where Earth people and Home Planet people had teamed up. The man called Rob was from Home Planet, but he had been wearing a laboratory security tag. He was one of the team.

Through some highly illegal hacking, back on Four Eighty-One, she'd found out about the EarthAid project. She knew it was to be an undercover operation. No-one on Earth was meant to know that people from Home Planet were there. But it was obvious that some Earth people – even if only a select few – were in on the secret. Logically then, those few would know about the globe-ringers, how many there were – and where they were.

And if scientists from Home were working with Earth scientists, they would likely possess the technology to trace each shoe. The question was, if she and Ridd stole a globeringer, would the laboratory team be able to track it down? Immobilise it? Destroy it? The only way they could stop them doing so would be to search out and destroy any Home Planet technology inside the lab.

As she thought about ways she could break in without being caught, the word 'destroy' seemed to repeat itself in her brain. She didn't know how tight security was inside the lab. She could risk breaking in and being caught in the act of sabotage. Or, she could simply burn the place down.

But to do that, she would have to go shopping...

*

Later, much later, she returned to the laboratory. She had stolen a car from outside someone's house and left it in a car park in the nearest town. It would have been fun to have been able to stroll round the shops, but they were practically all closed. Bel selected a high-class restaurant which served vegetarian food, and ate dinner, while she studied a map of the local area. She then visited a late opening supermarket and bought a carrier bag full of ingredients.

"Making a cake, are we?" said the young man at the check-out, attempting to be friendly.

Bel gave him a frosty smile. "No, we're making a bomb..."

She stole another car from a pub car park and made her way back to the lab. On her way, she stopped at a service station – she wanted petrol to take away in a container. The woman behind the counter told her she must have a plastic, regulation, safety container. Stifling her impatience, she bought one off the shelf in the service station shop and went to the pumps to fill it. Having paid for both items, she drove back to the laboratory, parking in deep shadow a short distance away.

For Bel – who was quick, quiet and deadly efficient – it was about an hour's work to prepare and plant the device which would cause the degree of devastation required. She disappeared back into the darkness and leaving the laboratory grounds, returned to the car. Through the open driver's window, she pointed the probe. The first signal she sent set off the fire alarm. There weren't many people in the building but she wanted to give them a chance. It was equipment she was out to destroy, not people. Ridd would have had no such scruples. But she was Bel. Underneath the layers of ice there remained a streak of compassion.

The second signal caused a muffled explosion at the back of the building. She waited until she could discern the orange glow of a fire, well started, having distributed enough petrol to ensure that it took hold. Using the route she had planned over her dinner that evening she headed for Hollybrook. Of course they would discover that someone had used a bomb to start the fire. But they would never find her. Ridd would have commandeered the globeringer by now and by tomorrow they would be re-masked – and far away.

During the short drive, two fire engines passed her, heading in the opposite direction – lights flashing, sirens blaring.

"You're too late," she said, watching them in her rear view mirror, as they disappeared round a bend.

*

Whilst Bel was engaged in her destructive work, Ridd was hiding deep within the darkened shrubbery at the

188

edge of the field where the shoe was. He gazed upon it with a dark, unblinking stare. He had seen Stacey run toward it after it had re-masked from helicopter to caravan. They should be moving soon. He calculated that there had been enough time for Stacey to be re-united with her mother – and all that sentimental muck humans went in for.

He knew Bel had eaten at the restaurant. Since they had become a team, he and she frequently checked each other out, mentally. But he hadn't eaten since their early breakfast, and was feeling decidedly empty. He popped a couple of food pills and waited for the hunger pangs to go away.

Ah! After an unbelievably long wait, the shoe began to move. It passed quite near to him, bumping gently over the uneven surface as it drove out of the field and into the lane. It was up to the girl now, and she wouldn't let him down – she knew the score. Her mother would have to leave the globeringer to get back to her house. Once out of the shoe, she would be wide open for attack. Unless Stacey got all the crew out, leaving the shoe empty – and his for the taking – he would strike.

## Chapter Thirty Six

**MUM'S RETURN**

Rob had been in touch with the watch crew on the far-reacher and told them what they had found out from Stacey. Could they account for the presence of a Home Planet criminal on Earth? Had there been a break from the penal planet? Watch captain got back to them about twenty minutes later. Yes there had been a break from Four Eighty-One. The description they gave fitted the old man, who was known as Ridd. He had a woman accomplice known as Bel. The far-reacher had received sets of their personality prints from the prison authorities.

The orders were for Rob, Ean and the children to leave the shoe – some time within the next hour – as if playing into the old man's hands. The watch crew had a lock on the shoe – tuned to the highest sensitivity. As soon as Ridd and Bel had taken possession, their personality prints would appear on the G5 screen in the far-reacher. From outside Earth's atmosphere the shoe would be sealed, rendered invisible – and lifted back to the host ship. The shoe's inside temperature would be drastically reduced, causing hypothermia. By the time Bel and Ridd got to the far-reacher, they would be unconscious and ready for putting into stasis. Back on Home Planet, a prison ship would be waiting to return them to Four Eighty-One.

Genno had volunteered to bring the globeringer back to Earth to collect Rob and the children. In the time it would take to achieve this, they must stay put – and stay low. All globeringers were being recalled, they were told. Some successful mind-locks had taken place, but there had been all sorts of minor problems. The children were leaving too many traces – not just in Hollybrook – and it was becoming urgent for them to leave...

In the meantime, they had to park in the horse field next to the Farr's house. Stacey would have to return home first, pretending that Miss Wilson had just dropped her off. Not too long after, her mum would have to arrive. Then a little after that – Rob and the children.

"How are we going to arrange this so that it looks natural, Stacey?" asked her mum.

"You should ring dad on that gadget." She nodded at the shoe link, "and prepare him for your sudden return home. He'll be so happy, mum!"

"Hmm... we didn't part on very good terms..."

"I think he'll just let all that stay in the past. Mum, believe me, he has missed you like crazy. He has been so unhappy without you. We all have."

Ean bit her lip and picked up the shoe link. Rob told everyone to shut up while Ean made her call. As Stacey heard her dad respond to her mum's voice, she started to smile. She could hear him exclaiming with disbelief and more than once heard him demand, "Where have you *been?!*"

Of course, most of the conversation was one-sided. "I

couldn't ring! I couldn't write! It was impossible!... No, I can't say why over the phone, Peter!"

Mab exchanged glances with Brod. *"It makes you realise what she gave up for a year – doesn't it?"*

*"Yeah...."* Brod answered *"She's got some guts, hasn't she? Rob told me she had been made an Honorary Home-daughter."*

*"And well deserved. I've just realised how much we'll miss her. D'you think we'll ever see her again?"*

*"Yep,"* said Brod, who didn't want to think of life without Ean.

The one-sided conversation continued. "Darling, listen, I have some friends with me – a teacher and four school children. They've been part of the project. Can we extend some hospitality to them? No, they'll be sleeping in the caravan, but they're a bit low on food... " (Of course, the shoe was not going to be there by the time Rob and the children had eaten supper at the Farrs, but Peter Farr didn't need to know that just now.) "The freezer is reasonably well stocked, is it...? Oh great... ! Give my love to Stacey and Jonathan." She winked at Stacey. "And tell them I can't wait to see them... We're not far away, I should be home in about twenty minutes, half an hour... " (They were in fact, only down the lane a little way but she wanted to give him time to adjust to her sudden arrival.) "Yeah, I know I should've let you know sooner, but it was impossible... Why? Well... er there was... a sort of communications block!" Ean screwed her face up, knowing how feeble her excuse sounded. "Peter! No more questions! I'll be seeing you shortly and we can talk!"

The return had begun – as well choreographed as a

ballet. Stacey arrived home first, pretending Miss Wilson had dropped her at the end of Mulberry Lane. She reacted to the news of her mum's imminent return with what she hoped was a realistic display of joy. Happily, Jonathan was so excited that he eclipsed her completely, and she just ended up smiling stupidly.

From being in a state of shock, her dad suddenly launched himself into action. Lugging the vacuum cleaner into the living room, he plugged it in. "I'll just give it a quick whip over. Stacey, tidy those school books off the floor. Jonathan, take your football boots upstairs and put your kit in the wash."

They rushed around bumping into one another, as dad barked various orders. "Stacey, wash up those few dishes in the sink will you?"

Stacey did as she was told, grumbling under her breath that she hadn't had any tea, and why should she have to clear other people's teatime mess up? Jonathan was sent upstairs to wash his face and hands, clean his teeth and change into his pyjamas. But he never got his pyjamas on. The doorbell rang just as he was wiping his face – including some of the day's dirt – on the towel.

Dad gave mum a long, silent hug, murmuring "Liz, Liz... "

As she hugged him back, she was thinking she would have to get used to being called 'Liz' again, instead of 'Ean'. Jonathan came thumping downstairs and she turned to him, folding him in her arms and lifting him up, kissing him, exclaiming, "Oooh! How tall and heavy you've grown, my darling! What has daddy been feeding you?"

"Just the normal stuff!" said Jonathan, wiping her

kisses off with his sleeve as she let him down to the floor again.

Then Stacey came up to her mum, arms wide, grinning broadly – but for an entirely different reason. They shared a secret – at least for the moment.

"So where are these friends of yours?" dad asked reluctantly, as he went to put the kettle on.

"They're in the caravan," said mum. "All right if I invite them in?"

# Chapter Thirty Seven

## HOME COOKING

Stacey was anxious for Rob and the children to come into the house. If Ridd thought she had not kept her word he might hurt her mum. Without waiting for her dad to answer, she added, "Yeah... if you two have finished snogging, let's call them in!"

Mum squeezed her arm as she slipped past Stacey to the front door.

"Mum! Let *me* go!" she whispered urgently, following her mum into the hallway. "That old man is out there somewhere! If he sees you he might hurt you!"

"Has it occurred to you that he might hurt you – if he thinks you haven't done as he asked?"

"Mum, stay here! I'm going to call them in from the back garden!" And before anything else could be said or done, Stacey had dashed through the kitchen and out of the back door.

Once out in the darkness, she took the clothes prop from the washing line – which still had stuff hanging on it. The shoe was now parked next to the hedge. Stacey reached over with the prop and banged on the door, shouting so that Ridd would hear her – and realise she was getting everyone out of the shoe. "OK YOU GUYS!

You can come in now!" For Ridd's benefit she added, "All of you!"

The caravan door opened to reveal Jay. The clothes prop was effectively pointing at his chest. He gasped with simulated horror. "Don't shoot! Don't shoot! I'll come quietly!"

"Stop fooling around, you nutter," Treo muttered from behind him. "We need to get out of this thing as quickly as possible!"

"Yes!" Rob agreed. "And we should walk round the front of the house – we need to be seen vacating the shoe!"

Stacey's response was to fling the prop on the ground and run back through the house to open the front door. As she passed through the kitchen, mum and dad were investigating the contents of the freezer. Mum stood up and raised an eyebrow at Stacey. "They're coming! I'm just gonna open the front door!"

Having found nothing suitable for vegetarians in the freezer, mum was bringing out lentils, rice, butter, onions and herbs.

Stacey made a face. "Mum! Just give them beef burgers!"

"Can't do that darling – they don't eat meat. You and Jonathan go in the other room and get to know your new friends. Dad and I will cook up a storm out here!"

Rob had been watching the food preparation and said, "Want me to take over? Peter might like to experience some real Home cooking!"

This offer, although meant in the kindest way, irritated Peter Farr. He didn't understand that 'Home' was a far away place, where they cooked food in new and different ways that he might like to try out. He assumed that Rob thought he couldn't cope with basic home cookery. "It's OK, thanks," said Peter, with cool politeness. "Liz and I will manage. It'll give us a chance to talk as well. You go and supervise the kids."

"Fine!" said Rob, sensing he'd put his foot in it. "I'll go and er... supervise. If you need any help, just call me!"

They ended up making what Stacey called 'lentil burgers'. Dad cooked a great pile of golden, crispy chips – his speciality – and mum made a salad. There wasn't much in the way of salad vegetables, so she supplemented them with apples from the fruit bowl, raisins and raw carrot.

Dad was surprised to see his daughter eat a plateful of food, after having already had tea at her teacher's house. But Stacey told him that it had only been a sandwich and biscuits – and anyway it seemed ages ago!

# Chapter Thirty Eight

**SUSPICIONS**

Peter Farr was overjoyed at his wife's return that Sunday evening but he was puzzled. For the past year, it turned out, she had been – not in the depths of some primitive jungle – but in New Zealand! So why hadn't she called? He would probably find out when they had some proper time alone together.

And why did he get the feeling that Stacey already knew Rob and the children? There was a look that passed between her and the girl called Mab, not long after they'd all been introduced. As if they shared a secret. Also there was a tension in the air that he couldn't quite pin down – almost as if they were expecting something to happen at any time. He remembered Liz telling him about Rob, the young New Zealand scientist who had come to work at Ferndean. So where had *he* been over the last year?

"I've been at Ferndean," replied Rob in answer to Peter's question. "They are doing valuable work there. I learned a lot – and I think Ean, er, Liz sorry, will have done the same during her stay away."

Peter decided he didn't trust Rob. He gave him a long, steady stare. "So, which part of New Zealand do you come from?"

"Dunedin," replied Rob, without hesitation.

"Is that where you all come from?"

"Thereabouts," answered Rob. "The kids returned with... Liz as part of a school project. We've promised to show them around the laboratory."

"Sounds like great fun to me!" Peter said, sarcastically. "Liz, we should organise something for the kids. Stacey and Jon break up on Tuesday. Couldn't we do something next weekend – something entertaining – together?"

"Er yes... good idea," said Liz, half-heartedly. But 'the kids' would be gone long before the weekend. In fact, it was likely they would be gone within the next twenty-four hours.

As soon as the two Home Planet criminals broke into the shoe it would be sealed and lifted by the watch crew on the far-reacher. With no shoe to accommodate them, Rob and the children would have to spend the night in the house. Where would they all sleep? Well, the arrangements might be a bit makeshift, but it was the least – and possibly the last thing – she could do for them.

Unlike his dad, Jonathan had taken at once to Rob, who treated him like a grown-up. Rob was tough-looking, with a tanned skin and the gleam of good humour in his eyes. Jonathan brought down his book on world wildlife, which included in its array of pictures, birds and animals now extinct.

Rob was very interested. He pointed to a picture of a Dodo. "We have lots of those where I come from."

"You can't have!" scoffed Jonathan. "It must be something else, 'cos those are *extinct*!"

Next, he took Rob outside to see his rabbit. "I call him Robbie," said Jonathan, pushing a piece of cabbage stump through the wire netting. The rabbit, who was already nibbling something, took no notice.

Rob quelled his feeling of disgust. There are no caged animals on Home Planet. No breathing thing is killed for its meat – or its skin. Between mankind and animal kind there is trust. Wildlife abounds. No need for zoos, no need for pets. Rob took a deep breath.

"That's Stacey's bushes you can smell. I'll show you!"

Rob followed the little boy across the garden.

"These bushes are magic! Stacey doesn't think they are, but they are. They stopped Fabian from crying – and Fabian cries a lot! And they made a dead kitten alive again. One day, I'm gonna be a doctor. But I won't have medicine, I'll grow these in my garden instead – and then I can make everyone better. Everyone!" With that, Jonathan grabbed a few of the small blossoms and tossed them into the air.

Rob grinned. "It's a great idea Jon, but you won't have any left if you don't treat them more carefully!" He was surprised at how well the leaves had grown. They were almost up to his waist – and flowering abundantly. Their fragrance reminded him of Home, and at that point he realised that one half of him was longing to return home, whilst the other half wanted to stay on Earth and keep helping.

Jonathan was tugging at his sleeve. "Rob? Can you show me inside your caravan?"

Rob sneaked a sideways glance to see if the caravan was still there. It was. There was no sign of life. It was a reasonable request. But the caravan had to be left strictly alone at this point. "Tell you what Jon. It's really late. How about I show you round in the morning?"

"But I've got to go to school in the morning!"

"I can show you before you go to school if you like."

"There won't be time! Please Rob – I only want a little look!"

"I really can't show you just now, Jon."

"But I showed you my wildlife book and my rabbit!"

"And I'll show you the caravan *in the morning*..."

"It's not the same..." grumbled Jonathan and walked crestfallen back to the house.

Stacey couldn't remember ever having enjoyed an evening so much, as she sat on the floor chatting with Mab and the others. The four alien children were friendly, lively – fun to be with. That's if they really were alien.... but how else could you explain the weird things that had been happening? Even after they had gone, knowing their stay was not going to be a long one – she would still have her mum. Life was looking up. But her life was already altered. She just didn't know it yet.

As if her mum knew what she was thinking, she came over and put her hands on Stacey's shoulders. "Do you realise how late it is? You should be in bed by now, getting some beauty sleep! So should Jonathan – it's way past his bedtime. Where is Jon, by the way?"

"I think he took Rob to see the rabbit," said Stacey, turning straight back to the conversation she was having with the others.

Liz found Rob still out in the garden. He was sitting on the old wooden bench.

"Where's Jonathan, Rob?"

"He went inside about ten minutes ago. He was in a huff because I wouldn't show him round the caravan. Well I couldn't very well, could I?"

"Not when it's about to be stolen by a homicidal maniac." Liz looked over to where the shoe's caravan shape was still outlined against the night sky. "Still there then. I wonder what he's playing at?"

"There are two of them remember. But I've only seen him."

"Do you think the woman was at the laboratory somewhere, while he was masquerading as the gardener?"

"Yeah, probably waiting out of sight until we were safely inside the lab."

"Rob, how d'you think they would have got inside the shoe, when it was sealed?"

"One of them is obviously an electronics whiz. How could they have broken through security on Four Eighty-One and stolen a ship, otherwise?"

Liz thought for a moment. "She wasn't with Ridd when he visited Stacey. I wonder where she was?"

"He didn't need her, did he? He just wanted to bend Stacey's mind a little."

"Poor little Stace, it's been a weird day for her. I told her to go to bed, but I bet she hasn't even moved yet. Which reminds me – I must go and say goodnight to Jonathan."

"Yes, and I'd better come in. I suppose it's only when we're all inside the house that they'll attempt to steal the shoe!"

Jonathan wasn't in bed. He wasn't even in his room. Liz checked the bathroom and the other bedrooms. She searched for him downstairs but he was nowhere to be found. She poked her head round the living room door and enquired of the company in general. "Has anyone seen Jonathan?"

There was a general shaking of heads and shrugging of shoulders.

Rob suddenly stood up. "I think I know where he is..." Peter wondered why his wife looked so horrified when he said, "He's in the caravan!"

# Chapter Thirty Nine

**JONATHAN**

He didn't think anyone would notice him go. Everyone was talking to everyone else. So Jonathan crept out of the front door, through the gate and along into the field where the caravan was parked next to the hedge. Somewhere in the distance he heard the sound of fire engines, but it barely registered – he was so involved in his exploit.

It was one of those motorised caravans – sleek and modern – although Jonathan couldn't see much detail in the dark. He made his way down between the hedge and the caravan and found a small set of steps leading up to the door. It was only at that point that he thought it might be locked. But it had been left open. It was dark inside. Jonathan began to talk aloud to himself because by this time, he was a bit nervous.

"I'll just see if I can find the light switch." At the word 'light' the interior lit up.

"Wo-ho!" Jonathan feasted his eyes on the most scientifically advanced caravan on earth.

The fact that the inside did not fit with the way it looked on the outside didn't even occur to him. At the end where the driver sat, a crescent shaped slice of dull metal on the end of a control column looked as though it might be a steering wheel. The console had no switches or buttons.

It was just a smooth slab with lots of detailed pictures on it – some of them were lit up. There were several small screens, but any instructions Jonathan might have been able to read were in a strange looking language. "Must be New Zealandish...." he muttered to himself. He noticed other doors. But before he explored further, he felt he would like to try one of the chairs. They were comfortable. He sat down, resting his hand on one of the arms. A table top glided out, stopping neatly in front of him, adjusting itself to his height. He put his head back. The table top slid quietly away and the chair lengthened into a bed, fitting itself round his small body. He could easily have fallen asleep right there and then, but he was far too curious.

A door near the back swished to one side, revealing a neat, shiny bathroom with two shower cubicles. Certain things responded to his presence as if they knew what he wanted. As soon as he peered into the mirror it lit up from behind, while a drawer opened beneath it, full of things for washing and brushing up. He poked his head inside a shower cubicle – and warm water instantly sprayed from the top and sides. It stopped as soon as he withdrew, but his hair and face were wet. "Wo-ho!" he said, wiping his face on his shirt. As he left the bathroom, the mirror light faded and the drawer closed.

The other door opened on a room that had no equipment in it at all. Jonathan thought it might have to do with making meals. The walls were lined with small compartments, each with a picture of a certain type of food on it. Some of the pictures were lit up. One lit-up picture was definitely an ice-cream cone. He was just wondering what would happen if he touched it, when he heard someone on the steps outside. Jonathan gasped with fright and put his hand to the door which closed smartly, hiding him from view.

*

Ridd was not surprised to find the light on in the caravan. Some vehicle lights simply came on as an individual approached. But he knew there was someone in the shoe. He sensed a child's presence – and where he was hiding. As soon as he was on board the shoe, he walked slowly over to the door behind which Jonathan hid. He put his hand out and the door whisked open. Jonathan gazed at Ridd with huge, scared eyes. "You're not Rob..." he said, his voice trembling. "Who...who are you?"

Ridd just stared, with his creepy, black eyes.

Jonathan shrank away from him. "This isn't your caravan," he whispered, "it's Rob's..." He could say no more. The old man's eyes seemed to bore into him. He was petrified, pressing himself into a corner.

Ridd's bony hand reached out and grabbing a fistful of the little boy's shirt, hauled him to his feet. Grabbing more shirt with his other hand, he lifted Jonathan until their faces were level. Jonathan was shaking violently. He was being sucked into the man's eyes. "You interfering little brat!!" he snarled.

A waft of air swept into the caravan as the door opened again. It was Bel. She had left the stolen car in the village High Street and walked down Mulberry Lane. She knew Ridd had just entered the caravan – he'd sent a message to her mind. As she entered the gate in the field she heard yet more fire engines. They couldn't put the fire out. Good.

But when she entered the caravan, her mood changed. She saw a small, terrified boy in Ridd's clutches, and knew he was doing him harm. With a howl of rage, Bel came up behind him. Clutching at his hair with both hands, she jerked his head back and kicked him viciously in the back of his legs. Ridd collapsed heavily onto the floor, and Jonathan rolled free. Scrambling for the open door, he fell down the steps and staggered towards the field gate.

*

As soon as he realised where Jonathan had gone, Rob ran out of the house closely followed by Ean. The quickest way to get to the caravan was to run through the back garden and scramble over the hedge. But as they crossed the garden, two things happened which stopped them in their tracks. A woman screamed. It came from the caravan – a long, agonized shriek.

Just as it was dying away, an electrical buzzing filled the air – and as Rob and Liz looked on, the caravan disappeared.

"It's been lifted already!" whispered Rob. "They didn't waste any time!" He turned to Liz, who stood there stunned, her face deathly white in the darkness.

"Jonathan! Jonathan's inside!!" she gasped, her legs buckling beneath her.

Rob caught her. "Ean! It's okay! He's still here! Ean! Ean!" He dragged her over to the bench and sitting her down, forced her head between her knees. "Ean! I can hear his mind! He's in the field! For goodness sake don't pass out – he needs your help!"

Stacey and the other children had run out of the front door. The meaning of Rob's sudden statement that Jonathan was in the caravan was not lost on them. Wondering what all the fuss was about, Peter followed more slowly. When he saw that the caravan had gone, he ran past them into the field. It hadn't driven past the front of the house. Although it was dark, he felt sure he would have seen or heard something. Had it been driven across the field, or further up the lane? He suddenly felt very sorry for Rob and the children. He would get the police onto it straight away.

It was then that he saw Jonathan. He was lying under the hedge, a smudge of white in the darkness. Peter ran to him. Had he been inside the caravan when it was stolen? Had the thieves thrown him out, before driving off? Was he badly hurt?

"It's all right Jon, Daddy's here! What happened to you, son?" He scooped Jonathan's small body into his arms.

Then the children were crowding round him. "Is he all right dad?" asked Stacey, in a frightened voice.

"Let's get him inside," said Jay, knowing Jonathan was in need of a special kind of medical attention.

As they were coming back through the field gate, Liz appeared with Rob. "Thank goodness! Oh, thank goodness! Is he hurt, Peter?" She leant forward, kissing Jonathan's pale cheek.

Brod and Mab pulled Stacey to one side where Jay and Treo were standing.

"Stacey, that creep has mucked his mind up. He needs Jay's help!" said Brod.

Jay touched Stacey's arm. "We need your healing leaves, Stacey – lots of them!"

A light switched on in Stacey's brain. He was referring to her beautiful bushes – and suddenly, amazingly, she knew where they came from. "They'll make him better, won't they?"

Four voices answered together, "Yes!"

As they made their way back into the house, Mab put a comforting arm round Stacey's shoulder.

# Chapter Forty

## DREAMS AND VISIONS

Once inside the house, Peter deposited Jonathan gently on the couch. "Liz get an ambulance – quick!" he snapped.

"We don't need an ambulance, Peter!" Liz said nervously.

"*WHAT!* Have you seen him? He looks *dead* for heaven's sake!!" Peter pushed past her and made for the telephone in the hallway.

Before he could reach it, Stacey had place herself squarely in front of him.

"Dad – we really don't need an ambulance. We can use the healing leaves. You know, from those bushes in the garden..."

"Don't be so ridiculous girl! Now get out of my way!" He pushed Stacey to one side and lunged for the phone.

As he keyed in 999, Rob came quietly up behind him and placing a hand on his arm, said quietly, "I'm sorry, Pete. I can't let you do this."

Peter turned furiously. He was conscious of two things at once: a desire to punch Rob in the face – and then an overwhelming desire to sleep. He looked down to where Rob's hand had been on his arm. He just had time to notice what looked like a white sticking plaster, before he collapsed senseless on the floor.

"Emergency – which service please?" came the operator's voice.

"I'm so sorry, there's been a mistake. My little boy has been playing with the telephone again." Rob spoke convincingly down the phone. "Sorry you were troubled!"

"You used an Arrestab? Rob, that was a bit drastic! Poor Peter..."

"It's only a short-term one Ean. It'll have worn off in a couple of hours. Remember what watch captain said, 'Stay put and stay low'! We can't afford to have blue flashing lights outside this address!" He bent over and started to lift Peter's body. "You go and see to Jonathan. I'll try and get him to bed – where's your bedroom?"

"Upstairs, first door on your right!"

The children had come in from the garden with a plastic carrier bag full of healing leaves. Their fragrance filled the kitchen. "Is there any way in which we can heat these really quickly?" Jay asked Stacey.

"We could microwave them," answered Stacey.

"Wouldn't that damage them?" Mab looked doubtful.

Treo considered the microwave oven very carefully, summing up how it worked. "If we warm them on half power for about thirty seconds, it should do the trick."

"We'll need something to put them in, so we can place the warm leaves under Jon's head." Jay looked at Stacey again.

"Pillow case!" Stacey ran upstairs, grabbed a fistful of clean pillow cases from the airing cupboard and ran down again. At the bottom of the stairs, Rob was waiting to lug her unconscious dad up to his bed. "What happened to dad?" Stacey gasped, but without waiting for an answer, hurried on into the kitchen.

Working quickly, they heated the leaves batch by batch and soon had the pillow case loosely filled. Before they could lose too much heat, they tied the open end up with string and put it inside another pillow case. Jay took the precious package into the living room.

Stacey's mum had been kneeling at Jonathan's side, stroking the hair back from his forehead. She moved aside so that the pillow could be slid under Jonathan's head. His face was deathly white. For one horrifying moment, Stacey thought he was dead. Then she noticed his chest rise and fall and felt a great surge of relief.

As they all crowded round, Jay was studying the patient very seriously. "Ean, you know – don't you – that the damage is mental? The healing leaves will make him peaceful but I would like to slip inside his mind if I may..."

Ean nodded silently. She had been crying and didn't dare speak, in case her voice broke on a sob.

Jay sat on the floor next to the sofa and closed his eyes. Jonathan's mind was like a black well – and he was falling down it. Jay summoned all his courage and swooped after him. Those watching him saw his head drop onto his chest. Chasing down the darkness after the tiny white figure, Jay forced himself to drop lower and lower, finally passing Jonathan, who knew only that he was plunging headlong into nothing. *"Hey Jon! It's me, Jay! Time to go home!"*

Jonathan opened his mouth and Jay heard the mental equivalent of a scream.

*"Jay! I can't stop!"*

*"Yes you can! I'm here – and you won't get past me!"*

Jonathan began to slow in his descent and as he and Jay came level, he reached out. Jay locked onto him, and using all his mental energist training, began the upward haul.

Jonathan clung on. He sensed that this was a dreadful dream from which he was not meant to awaken. But here was one of his new buddies – familiar and friendly. He felt his terror slip away as he was lifted towards the light. He said in an almost normal voice, *"Hey! I can see daylight! It's Stacey's garden, I can smell her plants!"*

*"That's right, Jon. They're healing leaves..."*

*"I know. They make people better. One day, Jay... I'm gonna be a doctor..."*

*"That's right, Jon, but we're nearly home now and I want you to sleep. When you wake up you'll feel so much better. It was only a bad dream Jon.... just a bad dream..."*

As Jay slowly rose to the surface of his mind, leaving Jonathan asleep, Rob came quietly back into the living room. He saw Jay's exhausted face and said quietly, "Good man, Jay. A job well done." Turning to Liz he suggested, "Why don't you sing Ean, er, Liz? Jon will hear you. It'll add to the calming effect of the leaves."

Ean began to sing. It was a lullaby she had learnt during her stay on Home Planet. To Stacey the words were a mystery – but they had a pleasant, soothing sound. The other children looked at each other and smiled. One by one they began to join in.

Stacey felt left out. *"Sing, Stacey..."* Mab's voice said, although Stacey didn't hear her actually say it – but she opened her mouth to sing – and the words were there.

Strange syllables came from her mouth, and she was singing the tune, which seemed as familiar to her as any of the nursery rhymes she had learned when she was little. Everyone found a comfortable place to sit, but Stacey sat on the floor next to her mum. She rested her head on the edge of the sofa, next to Jonathan's legs and still singing, closed her eyes.

The night sky full of stars was not a dream – it was a vision. The great blue planet that came into view was not Earth – but somewhere very like it. Beneath the cloud layer, there were mountains and hills, lakes and rivers, fields and forests. As she came in close, she seemed to be just above and behind a group of wild horses. They were on the move, their manes were flying, their hooves softly thudding as they fled. But Stacey knew they were not afraid. She knew they were glad to be alive – strong and free. Beyond them, the green slopes lay like welcoming arms. The horses changed direction, but Stacey's vision took her onward, toward a small community nestling at the foot of the encircling hills.

The dwellings here were all cylindrical – some tall, some short – their roofs like conical hats. Some buildings were bunched together, reminding Stacey of honeycomb. Every house was surrounded by flowers and trees. There were no fences. Cows, sheep, rabbits, ducks and geese wandered wherever they pleased. Stacey could see only natural boundaries, a line of trees here, a hedgerow there, a stream, a river. Then there were the windmills. Standing in clusters on the exposed slopes, their shell-like sails turned lazily in response to the summer's soft breath. It was beautiful...

"How can I sleep with you making that horrible row?"

Stacey suffered a rude awakening. Her brother was sitting up, yawning. His cheeks were bright pink and his eyes were sparkling crossly. Before he could say any more, mum, who had nodded off, woke up and gave him a huge hug.

"Mum! Leggo! You're squashing me!"

"Sorry, darling, but it's so good to see you back to normal." She glanced round and discovered that everybody, except Stacey, Jonathan and herself, was asleep. She lifted Jonathan off the sofa and said to Stacey, "While I put Jon to bed, will you go to the upstairs store cupboard and get all the spare blankets, pillows and sheets out that you can? We must make our guests comfortable for the night. For goodness' sake, it's two o'clock in the morning!" Then as an afterthought she added, "I don't think either you or Jonathan will be going to school today!"

# Chapter Forty One

## THE WHOLE TRUTH

They were all sorted out. A double airbed, spare mattress, sofa, pillows and cushions – everything Stacey and her mum could lay their hands on went towards giving their visitors somewhere soft to sleep. Finally, Stacey flopped into bed – still fully dressed like all the others – and immediately fell asleep. Liz slipped into bed next to Peter, who was snoring loudly. She didn't think that would keep her awake. Nothing could.

But she was mistaken. She had just laid her weary head on the pillow, when the telephone rang. "Who on earth is that?" she muttered crossly, as she grabbed the phone by the bed before it had chance to wake anyone else up. It was Professor Fairchild, the Head of Science at Ferndean. "Elizabeth, is that you? It's Barnaby Fairchild. I know you've been trying to get in touch with us..."

"Barnaby, I know we need to see you, but so much has happened. Can't it wait 'til morning? I'm absolutely shattered!"

"You must be, you poor dear. But you know I wouldn't call at this time unless it was urgent. Elizabeth, I have some dreadful news... the police called. There's been a fire at the laboratory..."

"A fire?" Liz sat up, suddenly wide awake. "How bad?"

The professor sounded near to tears. "Very bad Elizabeth... it's been gutted."

"Oh *no!*" Liz's hand went to her mouth. "How did it happen, d'you know?"

"Foul play, I'm afraid. Someone placed a bomb..."

"A *bomb!?* But why?"

He didn't answer. Instead he asked, "Elizabeth, are the children with you? And where is Rob?"

"All here. I can't tell you over the phone what's been happening, Barnaby. The er, vehicle was stolen..."

There was silence from the other end. Then, "Intercept?"

"No. I can't talk over the phone, Barnaby."

"Of course you can't. Elizabeth, I'm sorry about the ghastliness of the hour, but I'm coming over this very minute. Get some strong coffee brewing!" He rang off.

*

Liz woke Rob and went to put the kettle on. When Professor Fairchild arrived the three of them sat round the kitchen table to talk, as all the other rooms were occupied by sleeping bodies. The professor told them about the fire, how extensive the damage was and what – or who caused it.

Liz gasped. "It was Bel!"

"Who?" asked the Professor.

"Home Planet criminals... " added Rob, "trying to hijack the globeringer. It is highly likely that they are the ones who sabotaged the lab!"

The professor's mouth hung open. "What? How... how the devil did they get to Earth?"

They brought the professor up to date on everything that had happened since the globeringer touched down in the car wash last Thursday. Rob explained how complicated matters had become when two alien criminals had appeared on the scene.

"And you think they were responsible for the fire?" asked the Professor.

"Without a doubt," replied Rob. "They must have followed us to the lab. Knowing who we were, it wouldn't have taken much for them to work out that there were certain Home Planet facilities there."

"Hmm... yes, of course if they had stolen the shoe, we could quite easily have traced them!"

"And they weren't going to risk that!" added Rob.

Suddenly Peter poked his head round the kitchen door. He couldn't remember how he got to bed. He had woken up with a headache and come downstairs for tablets, to find a conference going on in his kitchen. Once more he had cause to be annoyed. "Is this a private party? Or can anyone join in?"

"Oh, Peter! Did we wake you up? Sorry!" exclaimed Liz and as the professor rose to his feet, "You've met Professor Barnaby Fairchild – my boss – haven't you?" Peter recognised the tall, grey-haired, rather distinguished gentleman and stepping forward, shook hands with a polite smile.

"Peter, there's been a fire at the laboratory!" Liz explained.

"No way? How bad?" He was shocked.

"Very serious, I'm afraid. Years of research gone up

in smoke. We have to properly assess the damage as yet, but that can really only be done in the daytime."

The professor took his glasses off and rubbed his eyes.

"We were making some serious progress too!" said Rob, stifling a yawn. Professor Fairchild addressed Peter. "Sometime very soon, we were going to hold a meeting in your wife's honour. She has to give us her report about the year she spent... er... in the field..."

"Oh yes, New Zealand!" answered Peter in a voice that clearly said he didn't believe it.

"Oh, it's still New Zealand is it?" The professor peered at Liz. "Haven't told him the truth yet, eh, Elizabeth?"

"Barnaby... I arrived back home only hours ago. And since then, there has been no time – what with preparing food for everyone, the globeringer being stolen, Jonathan getting hurt and then having to prepare beds for everyone... "

"Hey!" interrupted Peter. "I forgot! How is Jonathan?"

"He's fine, Peter. He's upstairs in bed if you want to go and have a look."

Peter put both hands on the table and leant toward his wife glowering. He said quietly, "Yes, Liz – but there was something pretty drastically wrong with him – how did he *get* fine?" He studied all three faces, an eyebrow raised. Even more quietly he asked, "Another thing. How is it that I wake up in bed fully clothed, with no recollection of how I got there?" He suddenly spoke much more loudly, "AND WHAT THE *HELL* IS A *GLOBERINGER!?*"

There was complete silence. The professor cleared his throat, "Well, it's three o'clock in the morning – but there's no time like the present! We're bound to need Peter's help sooner rather than later. He needs to know the truth. Go and talk to him, Elizabeth. From what you've been telling me, it seems your daughter knows more than he does!"

Rob got to his feet and poured coffee into two clean mugs. "Go on, Ean.... Liz, you've had no time to talk to each other. Take this up to bed with you – and tell him the truth!" As they meekly left the kitchen, he added, "Although he'll soon be needing more than strong coffee!"

\*

"All right, Liz. Give it to me straight – the whole truth. Just what have you been up to?"

Liz sat up in bed hugging her knees, wondering where to start. "It was well over a year ago, when Rob came to work at the laboratory. You remember the brilliant young scientist from... "

"New Zealand, how could I forget?"

"Well, he's not from New Zealand – he's from another planet. Peter, he's... he's an alien."

Peter turned his head and looked his wife full in the face. Holding her gaze, he said, "Liz, I'm tired and I've got a headache. Could we cut short the funny stuff and get to the truth?"

"It is the truth, Peter. Rob and those four kids are from another planet."

"Yeah? How did they get here, may I ask? Oh, I have it. That motorised caravan of theirs is really a space ship. Silly of me, I should've known." He picked up a newspaper that had been lying on the floor beside the bed, adding, "Please note: I'm not listening!"

Liz snatched the newspaper from his hands and flung it across the bedroom. *"Oh yes you are!* Do you think that after having promised to tell you the truth, after all the weird goings on of tonight – and especially at this late hour – I would start playing games with you?" She placed her hand over Peter's and said very earnestly, "Peter, open your mind. Do you really think that we are the only intelligent life in the entire universe?"

## Chapter Forty Two

### GLOBERINGER FIVE RETURNS

Monday promised to be another glorious sunny day. But at 8 Mulberry Lane all was quiet. The curtains remained closed. Its occupants – fast asleep – were making up for a very disturbed night.

However, at a large service station some way north of Hollybrook, the manager's Monday morning was turning out to be far from peaceful. First, the newspaper delivery was late, then one of his staff had reported in sick and now he was having to deal with an irate customer.

"Is there a problem, sir?" he asked of a young man in overalls with a shaved head.

"It's the car wash. I paid for those flippin' plastic discs and I fed 'em into the meter, and nuffink's 'appened!"

"Well, it was working when I last checked, sir... and at least three vehicles have been through it this morning. Are you sure it isn't already in use?"

"Of course it ain't in use! I'm not blind! There ain't no cars anywhere near it!"

"If you'll just wait a moment, sir, while this lady pays for her petrol, I'll come out and have a look." He attended to the customer, then called to a young woman who was packing sandwiches into the refrigerated display. "Hayley, look after the counter a minute while I go and see what's wrong with the car wash."

"Right you are Tom!" Hayley replied.

Picking up the keys to the car wash mechanism, the manager accompanied his customer round to the back of the forecourt, where the car wash was. It was obvious straight away that it *was* in use. Spray was flying everywhere and as the sunlight caught it, rainbow colours shimmered. The two men peered more closely. The brushes were bending to the shape of a vehicle, and they could hear them slap-slapping away as they got to work with the washing solution and gallons of water. The problem was, it was difficult to see exactly what sort of car was in there.

The manager crouched down. He could see clear through to the other side of the car wash. To all intents and purposes the car was invisible. The customer got down beside him and looked. Then they glanced at each other uneasily. "Er... perhaps we should just wait until this one goes through."

The young man just stared at the car wash.

The manager swallowed hard. "Er, it's nearly finished. You're next!"

"Nah..." the customer retreated a few steps. "I fink I'll go somewhere else..." With that, he sprinted to his van, climbed in and drove away at top speed.

"Your money, sir...!" the manager called feebly. But the van had gone.

The manager walked round the forecourt – to the end of the car wash where the clean vehicle emerges, and watched as a dark green Jeep drove out with a middle-aged man at the wheel. Waving cheerfully, the driver steered the vehicle off the forecourt, and disappeared in a southerly direction. The manager stood staring after it, jingling the unused keys in his hand for a moment.

*

It was a well-known secret within Tom's family that his brother-in-law, Craig, worked for Intercept. No-one was supposed to mention it, but last night at a family barbecue he had casually asked Craig how he was enjoying his job. He was surprised when Craig grabbed his elbow and dragged him to the other end of the garden. "I've got something I want you to do for me, Tom," he had confided, fixing Tom with his pale blue eyes. "There have been some weird goings-on in your part of the world. The police always report unusual events to us. Earlier today three of their squad cars were after a family camper which was breaking the speed limit. Apparently it was doing speeds unheard of for such a vehicle. They followed it onto a disused airfield where it drove inside an old aircraft hangar. As soon as the police cars hit the runway though, its surface became as slippery as ice. Their drivers lost control – and by the time they got to the hangar, the camper had disappeared.

"Most of the incidents have occurred south of you, around Ferndean – and the nearby village of Hollybrook. There are people we pay to look and listen for us. We received a report from Hollybrook... something very strange happened on Saturday night to a bunch of kids." He gave the gist of what had happened to the Sprike gang.

"We have to investigate everything, you understand, however unlikely it sounds. Phenomena... that's what we're all about. And what d'you think of this...? Saturday's Gazette." Craig had produced a half-page of the local newspaper and tapped a headline which read:

"FARM WORKER BLAMES ACCIDENT ON
'SHAPE-SHIFTING' HAYSTACK"

Tom read about the farm worker who insisted that he had seen a haystack turn into a Land Rover. The sight had so unnerved him that he had lost control and driven his tractor into a ditch. There was a photograph of Watson with a bandaged head and underneath it, 'Mr Watson... seeing things?'

"Tom, you work right inside the area where all these reports are coming from. Would you keep your eyes open for us?" He handed over his personal card. Apart from his name and telephone number, it bore an emblem – a globe with the word 'Intercept' across it like a No Entry sign.

Tom now extracted the card from his wallet and headed for the privacy of his office at the back of the garage. Closing the door behind him, he picked up the phone.

\*

Genno had seen the manager gazing thoughtfully after him as he drove away from the garage, and had decided to re-mask. As he searched for cover, he raised Rob on the shoe link. Rob had already traced the shoe's location with his electronic pulse – the call came through on the same piece of equipment:

"Yo Genno! Welcome to Earth! Everything go according to plan?"

"Yes. Our two criminals arrived on board. I have to report though, Rob, that the woman was dead." There was a pause at the other end – then very quietly, "I think we heard her die. She must have shielded Jonathan. Frankly I'd much sooner have heard that Ridd was dead!"

"He won't get much pity where he's going. Who's Jonathan?"

"Oh, it's a bit long winded. I'll tell you everything when you get here."

"Fine. Er, Rob at the service station where I touched down, the manager showed a rather keen interest in me. I'm going to find a place to re-mask." As he spoke Genno was feeding information into MAD. He waited as an image materialised on its screen. It was a large truck and underneath, the information: 'For conveyance of alcoholic beverages – Beer Delivery Truck'. "Rob – you still there?"

"Yeah, Genno."

"Obviously you'll know it's me if you use the pulse. But I'm adding a visual to that. I shall be a beer delivery truck."

"Supplying Fine Ales to the Fox and Hounds?"

"What?"

"Name of the local pub – social drinking venue."

"Whatever! Allowing time for re-mask, and keeping within the speed limits, I shall be with you in about an hour – hour and a half."

Driving onto an industrial estate, Genno found a row of garages. Picking an empty one, he drove inside and closed the door. A few minutes later, the door re-opened and a beer delivery truck backed carefully out.

# Chapter Forty Three

**GIFTS**

As Genno made his way south toward Hollybrook, people in the Farr household – apart from Rob, who was already up – were beginning to rise. When Peter entered the kitchen, Rob was busy washing up the coffee cups.

"Ah! Good morning, Peter! Coffee?"

"No thanks – I drink tea first thing. But help yourself."

"What, to coffee? No thanks. Don't drink it." Rob opened the oven door and a wonderful smell of baking bread wafted out. "I'll make you some tea though – that's something I do drink! And I've made some rolls. Fancy one?"

Peter was lost for words. A bread-baking alien was staying in his house. Honestly, he was dreaming, wasn't he?

"No, you're not dreaming," Rob commented cheerfully, as he picked each piping hot roll off the baking tray and placed it onto the cooling rack.

Peter was trying to be open-minded, but it was difficult. He found that what he had believed in the night was rapidly becoming unbelievable in the cold light of day. "Liz says you will probably have to return home today," he said, trying to sound natural.

"Well, we will probably depart today. The globeringer – Liz explained the globeringer thing?"

"Liz explained everything... everything!" Peter yawned cavernously.

"Well the globeringer has already touched down – "

"In a car wash," added Peter.

"Yes. I've spoken to Genno, my colleague, on the shoe link – that's our version of a mobile phone. The shoe will probably come and park in the field next door, same as before. Suitably masked, of course."

"Of course." Peter accepted a cup of tea and a hot roll with butter melting into its cut surface. He sipped at his tea for a moment or two then he said, "Rob," realising it was the first time he had used Rob's name. "Bear with me, will you? How do I know that all this alien stuff is not just a massive hoax? I must believe what Liz told me – she's deadly serious – but I'm finding it very difficult."

Rob came and sat opposite Peter at the kitchen table. "Yeah, I can understand that."

"Suppose everything you say is true," Peter continued. "You must understand why I feel angry. Liz has been away for a year without telling me where she was. I never stopped worrying about her. The kids have been unhappy – it's been the worst year of my life."

"Well it's over. There are no secrets anymore. You can do nothing but move forward. You have a gifted family. Another year from now and things will be so different for you."

Peter wondered what Rob meant by the expressions 'gifted' and 'so different' but before he could ask, Rob suddenly became business-like.

"We shall be gone in a very short time. While we are

still here, Home Planet technology is at your disposal. Is there anything I can do for you?"

Peter shook his head, smiling. What did Rob mean by 'Home Planet technology'? Could it provide him with extra money? A new house? A new car even?

"No it can't." Rob was shamelessly reading Peter's thoughts again. "But we can help you with your car. I'll call Treo." He stared at the ceiling for a moment.

The kitchen door opened and Treo walked in. "You want me for something?"

"Yeah. Glad you're awake!"

"Been awake for ages actually! Jay and I are helping Stacey and Ean... Liz, sorry – " She glanced at Peter." – to fold blankets and sheets and get the place tidy, Brod's using their vacuum cleaner and Mab's in the shower. Oh, and Jonathan's still asleep." She sat down next to Rob and opposite Peter. "Oh, by the way Mr Farr, Peter, whatever – I can do wonders for your vacuum cleaner if you want me to!"

"Thank you so much, Treo," said Rob sarcastically. "It's not the vacuum cleaner we're interested in at the moment – it's the family car!"

"Really?" replied Treo, brightening up considerably. "D'you want to show it to me?"

Within the next hour, Peter learned more about his car – and more about mechanics than he thought was possible to cram into such a short space of time. The volume of Treo's knowledge, as she slid underneath the car, or got her head under the bonnet, astounded him. She explained things in simple terms – and with a quirky humour that often had him laughing.

The morning had warmed up considerably and Mab

came out with fruit juice for them – and the bread rolls which Peter had never got round to trying. Treo and Peter sat in the front seat of the car for their break. Peter sighed. He was very impressed. The kid could easily be an alien. She was abnormally clever. They were all abnormally clever – and what with that unnerving habit they had of reading your mind – well, it made you think.

In spite of the fascinating company though, he was feeling shattered. His disturbed night was catching up on him. He didn't intend falling asleep just yet – he wanted to take his newly tuned car for a short test run. But he couldn't help closing his eyes...

*

Meanwhile, back inside the house, the aroma of freshly-baked bread had awoken Jonathan, who came downstairs demanding to be fed whatever it was he could smell. He was given breakfast, checked over by his mum and – being pronounced sound in wind and limb – was sent to join Mab and Stacey in the garden.

Brod collared Liz in the living room, saying he needed to talk to her. "Ean, you know when I left the horsebox and went for that disastrous stroll?"

"Brod, you don't need to apologise. You were under a lot of stress. We all were!"

"Well, much as I am sorry, apologising is not what this is about." He appeared distressed.

"Brod, what is it?"

"I lost my gift. Ean."

"What do you mean?" queried Liz, thinking that she probably knew what he meant.

"We're leaving today – I've found no-one with whom I could perform a mind-lock – "

"Brod, of all you young ones who've visited Earth, less than half have managed to perform a mind-lock. It can't be helped. Your assignments have been cut drastically short."

"It's not that, Ean, what I'm trying to say is, that even if I had the time – I couldn't do it. That criminal gutted my mind. I can think and behave like the rest of my group, but I no longer carry the gift I was sent to Earth with."

He looked so sad and solemn that Liz gave him a big impulsive hug. Then with her hands on his shoulders she peered into his face saying, "You feel as though you were entrusted with something precious – and you betrayed that trust, is that it?"

"That's just about it."

"Brod, you were the victim of a crime, for goodness sake!" Before he could interrupt her, she carried on. "Look, when you get back home, there'll be a long de-briefing session. You will all have the chance to meet with one another and talk about your mission. Do you think all the experiences related will be good ones?"

"No, I don't suppose so."

"Of course they won't be. There are bound to be some who have good things to tell, but there will be many who've been disappointed, many who've had frightening experiences – like you. On the other hand, some experiences might be hilarious! And you know what, Brod? The EarthAid Committee will want to hear every single story. And they will be so proud. Proud that you had the courage to come. Proud that you had even limited success. They can learn from your experiences – and use that knowledge when they make their next attempt to help us poor Earthlings. One of the Home Planet scientists told me before I left that they would never stop trying to help us. And they can only succeed if they have brave people like you!"

There was a slightly embarrassed silence. Liz resorted to examining her fingernails. When she looked up, Brod was grinning broadly at her. She grinned back – and they both burst out laughing.

*

Jonathan had let his rabbit out and was playing with it on the grass. Mab and Stacey were cutting sweet peas. They already had two large bunches. Stacey was trying hard not to think about Rob and the children's imminent leaving. She said, "We only met yesterday didn't we? And yet I feel as though I've known you forever."

"There's a reason for that, Stace." Mab sat on the bench and put her bunch of flowers on the grass.

Stacey did the same.

"We children didn't come to Earth with your mum just for the experience. I know we talked a lot last night about the different way we have of doing things – and I learned a lot about how people on Earth manage their lives – what makes them tick."

"I did think that was the reason you came. To sort of pick up knowledge of us, because we're like you."

"Yes, it's as if our two planets are related to each other. But what makes us totally different is our histories, I guess." Mab stared at Stacey and then burst out laughing.

"You're reading my mind again!" Stacey punched Mab on the arm. "What's so funny?"

"I just saw a parade of kings and queens pass through your mind – I didn't mean *that* sort of history! I meant our environmental histories."

"Oh yes, of course," Stacey said sadly. "We've ruined the Earth, haven't we?"

"Almost. But when we were taking Earth studies back at Home, we learnt that the serious bad stuff only happened within the last century – the last fifty years even. The thing is, young people are stuck with what the previous generations have done – and there's no way back."

Stacey gazed at Mab. "I know what you came for. To help us find the way back." She smiled. "How are we gonna find the way back, Mab?"

Mab smiled. "You tell me, Stacey Farr."

Stacey closed her eyes. "Let's see. You came here to deliver gifts. Mental gifts. You each came here to find someone special with whom you could perform a... a... mind-lock. This is the way the gift will be passed, from one of you, to one of us. These gifts are to be given to young people – like me – so that, with what we carry in our minds, we can change the shape of the future. Is that right?" Stacey found she was getting a headache – but there was something very important she needed to find out... "Did you mind-lock with me, Mab?"

*"I did, Stacey."*

"What gift have you given *me*?"

*"You are using it right now, Stacey... you are reading my mind."*

Stacey's eyes flew open.

*"How else could you have answered your own question? You picked the information right out of here!"* Mab tapped at the side of her head with her knuckles, then went back to normal speech. "Of course, it will give you a headache to begin with, but you'll overcome that."

"But how did you do it? And why? How will reading people's minds help with Earth's future?"

"Firstly, Earth people should be able to mind-read. Somehow, very early on in your planet's history, you lost the ability – we don't know why. I just altered something slightly in your brain. You were a good subject for it. I was told I would have to mind-lock with someone having the right brain pattern, someone sensitive. You were a pushover!"

"When did you do it?"

"You *know* when I did it!"

"That song! When we were singing to Jonathan!"

"Yes! And to give you a gentle start, I sent you a vision..."

"The horses... "

"Yes, and the village – that's where I live!"

"It's beautiful, Mab... I wish I lived there."

# Chapter Forty Four

Robbie the rabbit had found a wonderful, warm spot under the healing leaves and was enjoying a deep, fragrant slumber. Otherwise he might have bolted at the sudden invasion of the garden by what seemed like a crowd of people.

The professor had turned up again and Rob was eager to show him the healing leaves. Ean, Brod and Jay followed them out into the sunshine. The professor approached the plants with an almost worshipful air. "Will you just look at these little beauties!" he exclaimed in a hoarse whisper. He got out a small pair of secateurs and expertly snipped off a sprig. "Oh ho! Smell that!" He held it to his nose. "When did you say they were planted?"

"Stacey? When did you plant them?" asked her mum.

"Er, last Thursday – after school."

Professor Fairchild came over and crouched down in front of where Stacey was sitting. "Now then, young lady, you did a magnificent job of planting those seeds."

Stacey didn't like the professor. He may have crouched, to be on her level but he spoke to her as if she were a five year old. "It wasn't magnificent. I only put them in the earth. And I planted them because they were ready to sprout."

235

"But only look how well they've grown!" he exclaimed. "And that has to be your expert touch, young lady!"

Stacey stared rudely back at the professor.

He stood up slowly with a little groan, muttering that his knees were playing him up again. As he did so, Stacey thought she would try out her new gift by reading his mind. She felt instinctively that she shouldn't, that she was breaking the bounds of good manners, but she couldn't help herself.

What she understood from his thoughts was that he must be nice to this little girl, otherwise she wouldn't give him her plants. He hobbled over once more to where the healing leaves were growing. With a deepening sense of shame, Stacey hung around the old man's mind. She sensed his love of growing things and his joy over the existence of the healing leaves. Underneath that – and at this point, Stacey's head began to ache – he was grieving. Mourning the loss of something he loved. It was the laboratory. His research – his life's work.

She remembered her conversation with her dad on this very bench only a few nights ago. How the team of scientists under the professor had finally cultivated the tree with special characteristics. A tree that would help to green the scarred landscape of the tropical rain forests. It was her mum's life work too. And probably Rob's.

The professor's thought processes revealed that he had just been to the laboratory to see the damage for himself. The fire had been so devastating, it had destroyed everything. They were going to have to start all over again. They would need all of the special skills Elizabeth Farr had picked up during her year on Home Planet. And if Stacey could be persuaded to donate the healing leaves she had planted in her garden, that would give them a real boost as they began again.

Until the laboratory was rebuilt, they would find temporary premises somewhere, and carefully propagate the leaves. Wherever they were planted, they would promote growth, encourage wildlife – and purify the air. And last but by no means least, they had those phenomenal healing properties.

Stacey didn't realise she had shut her eyes until she felt a light touch on her arm. It was Mab. "Before everyone came into the garden, you asked me why I had given you the gift of mind reading. And how could such an ability possibly help Earth's future? Stace, you have just answered your own question. The professor would never have persuaded you to willingly give up those leaves. But by reading his mind, you have understood what a dedicated old man he is. He loves his plants, and before he dies, he wants to make a difference to Earth's future. The very next thing you do will help him to achieve that."

Stacey got to her feet, her head still pounding, her eyes watering. She went to the garden shed and got out her dad's cleanest spade. Before she got to where the professor was standing, he turned. His expression was a mixture of sadness and hope.

Stacey handed him the spade.

# Chapter Forty Five

**INTERCEPT**

Peter Farr grinned as he drove his newly tuned car along the village High Street. It was going like a bird – the engine positively sang. That lass certainly knew her stuff. What was really weird though, was how he'd nodded off as he sat in the car. That in itself wasn't strange – he'd had a terrible night and was still really tired. They all were. It was the way he felt when he woke up.

He'd been dreaming pleasantly and wondered where on earth he was. Then he remembered – they'd been working on the car. Treo had obviously decided not to wake him and had gone inside.

He had sat there, in the front seat of the car – the seven-year-old, well used family car – and felt as though he knew every single part of it. Every nut, bolt and wire. If something were to go wrong, he would locate the problem instantly – and be able to put it right. He could never normally be bothered with motor mechanics, nearly always ended up taking it to the garage for repairs and maintenance. But now, it was as if a hidden corner of his brain had contained the mechanical know-how all along, and someone had simply shone a powerful light on it.

As he headed for the main road out of Hollybrook, he was surprised to see that a police road block had been set up. They were stopping and questioning the drivers of all vehicles going in and out of the village. As he stopped at the barrier a policeman came round to his side of the car. Peter looked up through the already open window. "What's going on then, officer? Is there a murderer on the loose or something?"

"Not exactly, sir, but there's been a massive bank robbery and we've been tipped off that the gang has gone to ground somewhere in this immediate area. D'you mind if I ask you a few questions?" The policeman checked his clip board. "Do you live in Hollybrook, sir?"

"Yes." Peter obliged by giving his address.

"Is there anyone actually at your home address at the moment, sir? It may seem irrelevant, sir, but it's all part of our safety check."

Peter stared straight through the windscreen, suddenly feeling extremely uneasy. "Er, just the wife.... and the rabbit," he laughed feebly.

He was asked if he had seen anything unusual, anything peculiar, not just today but over the last few days.

"No, life's just as boring as ever, I'm afraid," he replied, wondering how long this was going to take.

"What is your destination, sir?"

"Oh, I've just had my car serviced and I was taking it for a test run. I was thinking of doing the short drive to Ferndean and back."

"Under the circumstances, sir, I think you would be safer returning home if your journey isn't absolutely necessary."

"Things are that dodgy, are they? OK, officer. Hope you catch your robbers."

On his way back to Mulberry Lane, Peter stopped briefly to buy a newspaper. He didn't believe the police story but if there had been a massive robbery, it might be in the local paper. He parked behind a large, black van with shaded windows.

As he entered the shop, the shopkeeper greeted him cheerfully, "Morning, Mr Farr!" At the mention of his name a man wearing a baseball cap, who had been browsing through the magazines, glanced up and stared at him. Peter stared back but he couldn't see the man's eyes. He was wearing dark glasses. Slightly unnerved, he bought his newspaper and left. It was as he felt in his pocket for the car keys, that his mind registered what he had seen. The cap the stranger had been wearing bore the Intercept emblem.

He had to wait for a beer delivery truck to pass before he could open the car door and get in. He had a moment or two to study the black van. An array of antennae on its roof – darkened windows. It looked like the kind of vehicle he had seen on television whenever Intercept featured on the News. The police, and Intercept. They must be here for the return of the...what was it called?... globeringer. Maybe they weren't sure what they were here for, but they knew something big was brewing.

Peter was not to know that the bizarre experience of the Sprike gang had somehow come to the notice of the ever-watchful Intercept. That their attention was already focused on Mulberry Lane.

The beer delivery truck was some way down the High Street, and as there was nothing else coming, Peter pulled out, thinking he must get home and warn Rob and the kids. In his wing mirror he saw the man wearing the baseball cap come round the van and climb into the driver's seat. There were two other men sat in the front. He gulped down his growing panic. How many, Peter wondered, were crammed in the back?

## Chapter Forty Six

**DON'T TALK – RUN!**

Genno, driving the beer delivery truck – and remembering the name 'Fox and Hounds' – had convinced the police at the road block that he had a delivery to make at the pub in Hollybrook. Almost as soon as he had left the road block, the soft, electronic voice of MAD spoke up: "Detect Intercept presence – shield is in place – proceed with extreme caution."

"Thank you MAD," said Genno, a few seconds later driving past a sinister looking black van with shaded windows.

He knew where he was expected to park, because there was an on-screen map with the route marked all the way to the field at the end of Mulberry Lane. He got on the shoe link to Rob. "Genno. What's up?"

"Rob – I'm in Hollybrook – "

"Great!"

"Rob – Intercept is right here in the village."

Those in the garden watching Rob take the call saw his expression change – and knew there was trouble.

"Have they detected the shoe?" asked Rob.

"Not according to MAD. The shield is up."

"The sooner you pick us up, the better. Rather than

park in the field as planned, you'd better stop in the lane outside the house. From there I'll direct you to a place where we can lift-off without being seen."

"You hope!" replied Genno "I'm signalling right to turn into the lane. Go and get those kids!"

Peter, someway behind the beer delivery truck, saw it signal right and turn into Mulberry Lane. Then he said softly to himself, "Of course!" It was a very convincing beer truck, but there were no pubs down the lane. And another thing – it was a dead end. It must be that space vehicle in disguise. Peter shook his head. A strong sense of unreality was taking hold of him. Space vehicle!

As *if!* The delivery truck had probably taken a wrong turn and would soon be backing out. But in his rear view mirror, he saw that the Intercept van had pulled out and was following him. Had they come to the same conclusion as he had? He signalled right to turn into the lane. The van also signalled right. Peter broke out in a sweat.

Rob, Mab, Brod, Treo and Jay were waiting as the beer delivery truck jerked to a stop outside number eight. Rob wrenched the door open and virtually pushed the children on board. He was bullying them not to keep turning back to say goodbye. As Peter pulled up a few feet behind he could hear Rob say, "No time, no time. Just go, go, go!"

Before Rob could even shut the door, Genno was moving away, heading on down the track that led towards the open fields.

The Intercept van had entered the lane. Peter, who was now out of the car, did a sharp double take – a second identical van was close behind it. He felt an overpowering urge to try and stop them but as they accelerated towards him, Liz was suddenly there, pulling at his hand. She shouted, "Leave them Peter, leave them! The globeringer can take care of itself. Come on!"

"Where are we going?" he called after her, as she ran through the gate into the horse field.

"To say goodbye!" she yelled back. "Come on! Let's catch up with Stacey and Jon!"

An enormous thump, followed by a crash, caused Peter to whip round. The first van had come to a violent stop just outside number six – and the second van had ploughed straight into its rear.

"Don't stop Peter!" Liz had continued running across the field. "They've just crashed into a force field!"

"Wo!" Peter, running to keep up with her, sounded just like Jonathan. "That should hold 'em up for a while!"

"Only for a while, though," said Liz, climbing over a gate. "It uses practically all their power. The shoe won't be able to mask – and they'll have to shut down the force field before they can lift-off."

"Is that going to be a problem?"

"It'll take about thirty seconds from the time the force field is shut down to the time when they have built up enough power to lift-off. Unmasked."

"So we just have to hope that the vans have been put well and truly out of action!"

"Don't talk Peter – run!"

*

Stacey and Jonathan had got a head start in taking the short cut across the fields. Past the spot where Jon and

Ben had found the kitten, through a gate, and over a field of stubble they ran.

"Stacey... I heard mum and dad talking... in bed last night." Jonathan's voice wobbled as he ran. "Rob, Brod, Jay, Mab and Treo... are they... are they... from another planet?"

"Don't talk Jon – run!"

She knew it was likely that the globeringer would be gone by the time they got to its chosen point of lift-off, but she just... wanted to be there. Running through the field where the shoe had landed when it was a helicopter, Stacey had to stop for a moment – she had got a stitch in her side. This gave Jonathan, who was lagging behind, time to catch up. They went on through the trees, and up the slope to the top.

If Stacey's heart hadn't been pounding so loudly in her ears, she would have heard them coming. A line of military helicopters swept low, over the brow of the hill, the noise of their rotors suddenly filling the air. The two children instinctively cringed. Stacey grabbed Jonathan's hand, and bending double they scuttled upwards, knowing the shoe could not be far away. The roar of the helicopters subsided, but then it began to increase again as they gradually circled back.

At the top of the hill the children stopped. Down below in a field of standing grain was the globeringer. Unmasked, sleek, white – and shoe-shaped – with a row of windows near the top like lace holes.

"Oh, *that's* why it's called a shoe!" cried Stacey, laughing.

"Wo!" said Jonathan. They started running down the slope towards the field, but when they heard the overpowering beat of the helicopters returning, Stacey decided they were too exposed. Finding shelter in a clump of bushes, Stacey pulled Jonathan down with her. Through the leaves they watched the shoe.

It seemed to be moving. But it wasn't. It was shimmering, almost like a distorted image in a heat haze. The image began to dissolve. It wavered... and then the children were staring at an empty field.

As if trying to convince herself, Stacey said, "It's gone."

Without making a sound, Jonathan's lips formed the syllable, "Wo!"

*"Stacey! Use your gift well... It won't be easy at first... but you can do so much if you know what people are thinking... you won't be tricked by the words people say. With your gift you can negotiate... advise. Communication is the beginning of change... change for the better..."* And very faintly, the words entered Stacey's mind: *"See... you...again... "*

She was looking skyward, but of course there was nothing there. They really had gone. Mab had projected her thoughts Earthward for as long as she could, before they were finally out of range. She glanced down at the field again. Just where the shoe had stood, the grain had succumbed to powerful downward forces as it had lifted off. But that force had been so precisely controlled, it appeared as if a pattern had been cut in the corn. "Crop circles!" breathed Stacey.

The helicopters were hovering. The air vibrated. The first black van, its windscreen cracked and steam rising from a damaged engine, had arrived in the field just as the shoe disappeared. Its buckled rear doors practically fell off as men spilled from the back and began to advance to where the globeringer had stood. The second van, also badly damaged, came bumping into the field and slewed to a stop beside the first. From down the lane, came the sound of several police sirens. Stacey and Jonathan looked at each other and grinned smugly. They were all too late!

"C'mon," Stacey said, and they started back up the hill. At the top, their mum and dad emerged from behind some trees. Stacey could tell from her dad's stunned expression that they, too, had seen the globeringer vanish.

As they made their way home, Jonathan was gabbling. "It was a space ship wasn't it? And it just....just.... beamed up! Wo! Which planet do they come from mum? Can you show me on a map? Are they coming back? And can Brod n' Jay sleep in my room?"

Liz, who was feeling devastated, laughed in spite of herself. Scruffing the hair on the top of his head, she said, "Jon, it would be wonderful if they came back! But they've just had a very narrow escape." She put her arm round Stacey, adding, "One thing I do know. I shall never leave my family again. I missed you all so much!"

"Well, that's a relief!" said their dad, with a tinge of sarcasm.

They cut back across the fields, knowing that with all the attention focused on where the globeringer had been, no-one was likely to take much notice of them. As they got near to the house, dad began to whistle. It was a catchy little tune. Stacey glanced at Jonathan. They knew that when dad whistled, it meant he was plotting something.

"Family, I've been thinking!"

"Oh-oh!" was Stacey's comment.

"I think I've developed a flair for motor mechanics!"

There was silence. They were waiting for what was coming next.

"I was seriously wondering about the possibility of opening a car workshop – you know – for repairs and maintenance, MOTs, stuff like that. What d'you think, Liz?"

"Yes, dear, anything you like." Liz had gone back to looking sad, with a faraway expression in her eyes.

"I mean, people are always wanting help with their cars, aren't they? But although I like carpentry, I'm not half as busy as I would be, if I owned some kind of garage. Am I?"

No-one answered him. He wasn't in the least disheartened though. In fact, he became more enthusiastic as he imagined his dream becoming reality.

Liz glanced at him briefly and decided to humour him. "Where will you get the money from, love?"

"I've got a little put aside. But I could start doing repairs from the house. Liz, I know I can make a go of it!"

Stacey was gazing at her dad in wonder. She seemed to remember he had been outside doing some work on the car with Treo. Treo had come briefly into the garden, saying that she had left her dad asleep in the driver's seat. The thing is, if Treo had mind-locked with her dad, how could a knowledge of motor mechanics improve the Earth?

Her dad was still in full spate. "I can see us running a garage, with an excellent reputation. People will say, 'I always take my car to Farr' and, 'There's no better motor mechanic than Peter Farr'! They will drive away with their cars finely tuned – cleaned inside and out." He stopped walking, and as if he had just thought of it, he said

"Of course, it *might* mean installing a car wash...

# The End